BOOK ONE

INCA CURSE

The 4 Corners of the World Empire

ANDREW HARDY

2020

I was born just like a flower in a garden.
That's how I grew up.
Then came the age and I got older,
And when I had to die, I died
And I died.

INCA PACHACUTÉC
1438 to 1472

The Inca Empire, in South America, with the four regions that they call "Cornes of The World"

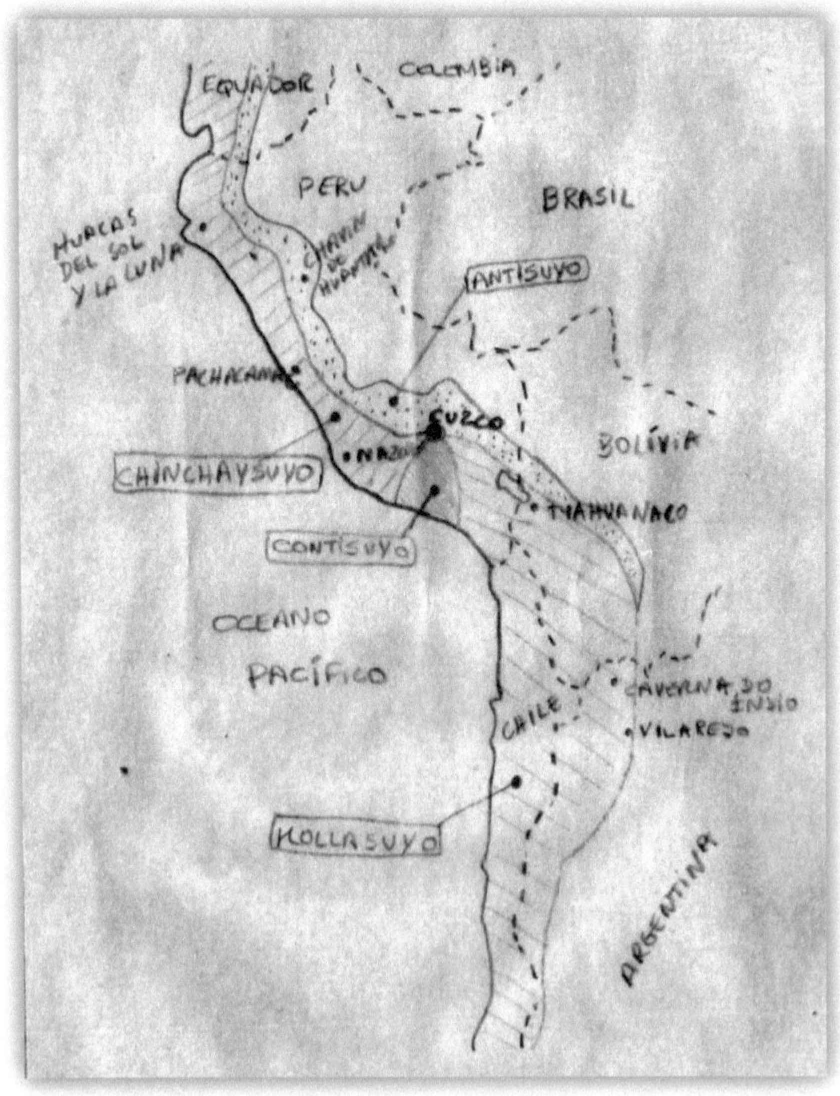

ONE

He was sitting on a very old sofa. A sofa that, at that moment, could not be judged by its age or appearance. The feeling he had was that it was one of the most comfortable where he had ever rested. Perhaps he had that opinion because it had been more than six hours since he had sat in a decent place. Not that he was! A place where you could really rest and recover from tiredness. He had made a not-so-pleasant trip: After he had landed at the airport, he had a lot of work to find a means of transport and complete his trip and, at great cost, found a bus that would take him where he wanted. He took the bus, which was going towards the North and the mountain range. It was full of farmers, mestizos and indigenous people. It was broken and stank of sweat and manure from some kind of animal.

A real calamity! He started to think that it would have been better to stay at home, where he certainly wouldn't have been through that kind of situation. Another big problem was his Spanish, which left a lot to be desired, which ended up embarrassing him, because he could not complain or interact at all. He started to feel very alone because of that. He had come here on a somewhat forced vacation, as he indicated his colleagues, claiming that he needed to see different things.

- You need to know the world! They said.

How did you work a lot, and in those days who didn't? In the end his hope was that such an opportunity could help him reorganize his thoughts, try to find answers to questions that in everyday life and, because this was very busy, he could not find. In a way he was excited. He wanted to release some of the stress that work and urban life caused him.

And so there he was, sitting on an old sofa, on the veranda of an Argentine friend's country house, wrapped in a blanket of Llama or Guanaco fur - he couldn't tell the difference between the two animals - that he had bought from a woman on the bus during the trip . The woman almost begged him on his knees for him to buy it, and embarrassed by the scene, he finally gave in. In the end, it was good, because the sudden drop in temperature made him feel happy and found that he had not done a bad deal. He was finishing preparing hot chocolate, but his camp stove was not very good, as the gas was running out. His friend's home had been an inheritance that was in process and had remained uninhabited for over ten years. He had recently received word that he had won the right to the property, but he needed to come to the site to take possession or he would lose it. Everything in the house was broken, because the things that were good had surely been stolen. He made a deal with his friend who would go there for free and in return would take care of the place, renovating the entire house and replacing the fence of the property. But I wasn't so sure I made a good deal.

He had a hot chocolate, not so hot, prepared in a hurry, watching the Full Moon move over the night profile of the mountains of the famous and beautiful Andes. I had never seen anything like it. It was beautiful! The Andean Moon was the most crowded I had ever seen. She seemed so close that if she reached out, she would touch her. The white of the Moon was mixed with the white of the tips of the mountains, almost making it seem that the two were one. And weren't they? I had read something some time ago about a theory of the Moon having formed from an impact on Earth. For fragments or something . But it didn't matter much at that moment.

It was the end of winter, but the combination of altitude and the fact that it was on the side of the great mountain range was still cold enough to freeze anyone who ventured there without wrapping up very well beforehand. A light mist began to form over the undergrowth that was around the house. Everything was very quiet. The situation was conducive to anyone's imaginative daydreams, let alone a person alone in an unknown and abandoned place. Every moment that passed he felt that he was involved with the environment in such an intimate way that soon he would no longer be surprised or admired that natural scene. In his mind, in his thoughts, the night gradually took a new direction: it became dark and threatening.

Perhaps he was having such a fearful interpretation of the night because his mood was very unsure about his future, or because he was not used to being alone. Without realizing it, he confused his state with the things that surrounded him. Suddenly he started to feel fear and insecurity. The darkness of the night, even though it was not so strong because of the moonlight, became a highlight for his fear. As much as he tried to think of pleasant things, everything he really saw at that moment: the moon, the night, the mountains, . They came like ghosts, to try to scare him, to take him from what he promised to be one of the only quiet moments he seemed to have found in his life.

Sometimes he managed to control himself, searching his memory for something that would give him comfort or pride. Anyway anything good to be able to feel a little more encouraged. But the attempts were all in vain. Minutes after being on these tireless searches and, finding nothing, he was overcome with anguish so great that he even had the chills of disgust for his mediocre life.

In front of the house there was a small lake, about fifty meters in diameter, which usually formed at that time as a result of the snow that melted from the mountain slopes and accumulated there. The house was further surrounded by a small forest with many medium-sized trees, but at night everything was difficult to confirm. He stared at the reflection of the moon, which was slowly forming on the surface of the small lake. His gaze was so fixed that he seemed to be looking at a television, where a special was happening about his own life. He considered his life a mere existence, because until that moment he had only survived, not really lived. He felt that everything he had actually done was not what he wanted for himself, but what others expected of him. They were of no value to him.

There was a dead tree to the left of the lake, and its shadow further emphasized that dark environment that was forming in his mind. He started to remember the folk stories he heard as a child. They were stories of werewolves, headless mules, witches, such scary creatures. Finally stories that, depending on the age at which they are heard, have a great power of persuasion. I thought they told that kind of story, most of the time, to make children more subordinate, more dependent on adults. His opinion was that this kind of thing should not be abused.

He rarely stopped to think about how much important information had been lost due to a principle that moves most people in the modern world: seeing and believing. Not only does modern man disregard the folklore of his people, he despises them and contributes to their extinction. When we lose respect for the culture of our people, we also lose a very important range of information that should be part of our critical consciousness, or sub consciousness. Many of the inexplicable things today could easily be cleared up if, in the course of history, certain people had not failed to tell others something they did not believe in. As a result, over time these losses have become greater and greater, perhaps due to the fear of exposing a different thought or situation that he has been through. Because everything that is alien to our daily life, to our limited life, to a safe daily life, almost always causes controversy.

He was called Victor and was quite reserved for the principles he defended. For this fact he was a very alone person. He even knew when he had exaggerated the defense of his ideals. He knew when he had been extreme, but unfortunately when he realized that, it was too late. In that way it always kept anyone who tried to get away. The cold outside the house was becoming unbearable. He had light brown hair, green eyes, and even though he was of northern European descent, he was not used to that intense cold. He had just completed his twenty-sixth birthday, but he didn't care much about this fact. It had been a long time since I had celebrated on that date.

Suddenly a wind started so strong that all the vegetation seemed to be dancing in honor of the Moon. The clouds that covered the sky moved quickly and passed the Moon as if they were afraid to stay in front of you. The fog had lifted.

He decided to go in to sleep a little, as he planned to visit the surroundings the next day very early. He went in and went to check if there was any wood so he could light the fireplace. To his disappointment he saw only a few sticks with a trace that had been burned a long time ago. He decided to sleep without lighting the fireplace. The bed was very old and was almost decomposing, full of termite holes. The sheet on the bed was grimy and smelled musty. If I went to sleep in that place, I would have to remove the sheet first. He held on to one side of the sheet and pulled, but he couldn't resist and tore. He took the remains that were left and heaped them near the fireplace. If you needed something to help start the fire, they would do.

He did a preliminary check to try to confirm that the bed would support his weight. In his view, the bed would support him perfectly, so he went to bed. He found it very comfortable and cozy. He considered it again because he had slept in so many worse places. It was practically paradise for him. After that exhausting day spent almost entirely on the road he would sleep in a decent place. But, when everything is going well, after two rolls to try to find a better and more comfortable position the bed creaked and was immediately followed by a breaking noise.

Suddenly he felt a chill in his belly, and when he realized it was already on the floor. He looked around trying to understand what had happened and realized that the bed had collapsed. He smiled and sighed, got up to fix it. As soon as he got up he realized that he was so cold that he started to shiver. He removed the mattress from the broken part of the bed and placed it on the floor so that he could sleep. It took him about five minutes lying down to realize that he would never be able to sleep there unless he lit the fireplace. He thought about burning what was left of the bed. But he soon concluded that it was crazy, because it would be easier to fix it the next day, than having to buy or build another one.

He wrapped himself in the blanket and, against his will, opened the door to go out in search of wood. He felt the cold air that came to receive him at the door, it was as if he had taken a push to return to the house. He was reluctant again, but he knew that the need for another source of heat inside the house was beyond his own will. He was used to accepting reality no matter how bad it was momentarily. He put the hesitation aside and left. He looked at the night sky once more. It had been about an hour since his last look. Even so, he felt alien to that landscape.

I had a feeling I didn't deserve to be there, or I couldn't be there. It was the feeling of being in a very special place. He was happy for an instant and didn't just want other people to see what he was seeing. He wanted other people to see things the way he did. In nature everything was so self-sufficient. Nothing there needed the human touch or the changes that the man brought. Sometimes he found himself wondering if man's evolution would have been really good .

Perhaps it would have been better to be stationed in an evolutionary track not so dangerous for ourselves and for other living beings. Many define man as a rational animal, but we have to accept that not all men are rational beings. Or even they are, as long as they are not subjected to experiences or situations that take them to the extreme of the human condition: the beginning of the animal condition. A man who loses his human condition can be worse than any wild animal we know.

He started to walk around the house to see if there was any wood needed to light the fireplace. He found it easier to find it in the back of the house, because in the films he had watched, usually the bundles were left there for burning. He found nothing, only the grass that grew beside the wall, which he would have to cut on the days he was there. Without having another option in mind, he headed for the forest, because there the probability of finding the much needed wood was greater. There are branches that dry and fall near the trees. The terrain was all rugged, covered with grass similar to that of African savannas, which reach at most knee-high. It was difficult to walk on the grass, due to the humidity that formed over it because of the night dew.

He got tired and decided to take whatever he found that was enough to spend the night, just so he could get back to the house faster. His fear had returned. I didn't even know what I was afraid of. But that feeling was different, I had never felt that. He looked towards the woods and it was as if someone or something was also watching him. He heard a noise. It was very low, but it was enough to paralyze him. He looked in the direction where the noise was coming from, but he couldn't see anything. He couldn't see very well and to make matters worse he was without his glasses. His vision was not yet adapted to the darkness, that is, even if there was anything there he would be able to see it.

He imagined it was just his mind. And after concentrating and thinking rationally, he calmed down. He advanced again towards the forest. But it was only a few steps before he could see a figure standing between a small tree and a rock. From the little he saw, he assumed it was very large and not human. It could be any animal. He was filled with panic, but he knew he should control himself. He started to walk slowly backwards, for he knew that any sudden movement could more easily attract the attention of whatever that animal was.

He managed to go back a few steps, but as he was walking on his back and, consequently, he could not see where he stepped. He tripped over an elevation of the terrain and fell on his back, but at no time did he take his eyes off the forest. To his misfortune, and even greater despair, the animal heard the noise. The animal immediately looked at him. Her eyes were a cherry red color and when she saw him they seemed to shine even more, as if meeting an old enemy again. He let out a grunt that seemed to echo the length of the great mountain range. As his cry passed, everything fell silent, as if all his life there had been extinguished. At the moment of the cry, when he opened his mouth, he could see the huge fangs being exposed.

Without thinking, he got up and ran towards the house, which was about fifty meters away. The sensation he experienced was of an animal being hunted, judged by the law of the jungle. The law where the strongest overlaps the weakest, which in this case was he. He heard the footsteps that followed him grow stronger and tried frantically to increase his pace. That was when he tripped over a small rotten log about three feet long. Acting on instinct, he picked up the trunk and turned to face the animal, as he knew he had no chance of escaping without a fight.

There was a surprise. The animal was no longer behind him. He remained just over twenty meters away. He seemed to be studying his future victim, knowing his weaknesses and strengths. If they looked again, for a brief moment, then the animal turned and walked towards the forest until it disappeared. Victor watched until the animal disappeared and, still walking in front of the forest, went back to the house. He was very confused and started doing things on pure impulse, or on instinct. I wasn't sure. After he felt safe, he turned home and ran again.

Rushed in. He threw the piece of wood on the floor. He took the broken parts of the bed and used them as backrests on the doors. I was still very nervous, but I was already beginning to act consciously. He sat on the mattress. Only at that moment did he feel a great pain in his right leg and when he looked at her he saw that he was bleeding. He thought it best to light the fireplace: the heat would not only help him against the cold, but also, in case the animal returned. You could use it to defend yourself, or chase the animal away. It was not very difficult to set fire to the trunk, as the tips of burnt sticks that were in the fireplace caught fire very easily.

He sat by the fireplace and began to doubt whether what he had been through was reality or not. He was beginning to believe that it had all been a dream, or because he was impressed by the location. But soon his doubt left him, because when he looked at his leg he saw that everything had been very real. He started to think, searching his memory and trying to remember how he had done that wound.

He didn't have a first aid kit, so he washed the wound with a little brandy he had brought to ward off the cold and dried it with a clean sock he had in his backpack, then using it as a bandage. He was very tired from the rush that night and the day he had. He took the opportunity to take a dose of his drink. He looked at his watch and saw that it was still very early, just after half past nine. He had done many things and time did not seem to pass as usual. He decided to lie down to see if, despite everything he had been through, he would be able to fall asleep. He kept his injured leg straight. He lay down with difficulty, but soon found a position not too unpleasant. He covered himself and remained in that position until he fell asleep.

He was standing facing the door of the house, but it was not the way he had left it. It was open! There was no more wind. There was no sound coming from outside. Everything seemed paralyzed. Suddenly he heard a huge growl. A hellish noise that seemed to cut his body in half. He was filled with dread and tried to hide, but his body was paralyzed. I couldn't move. He felt a huge pain in his leg, looked at her and saw that he was bleeding a lot.

He began to see the images around him passing by, as if he were walking, only without moving his legs. The rhythm of your heartbeat increased instantly. He wanted to remain still, but his legs did not obey. He tried to raise his hands in order to cling to something, but it was useless. He heard the horrible growl again. It was getting closer and closer, it seemed to become more real, more present. His despair was growing. He reached the other side of the house, which overlooked the forest. He looked in the distance and could see a huge figure that moved slowly towards him.

He looked at the figure, realized that it was looking at him, his eyes shone as if there were some kind of mesmerizing energy in them.

Something that seemed to catch the eye of the beholder. At that moment he sensed in his eyes that he feared for something, or feared something. But I wasn't sure about that. He thought it might be a tactic to approach without causing fear and then attack him by surprise. Slowly, the figure came out of the shadows where it was hidden. In the moonlight he can see something amazing, something he would never forget and never imagined seeing in his life.

His thoughts were lost for a long time, imagining many things that he could not explain, and he did not even know why he was thinking about them. When he came to, he realized that the supposed monster had stopped again. He was looking at him again. His gaze was still strange, but now it was as if he already knew him from somewhere. His fiery eyes penetrated her like a thrust with all his might. He felt like he was seeing an old friend again. Or rather: an old enemy. But something was not right. At this moment the animal turned its gaze to the sky, it seemed to be worried about something. Victor followed his gaze. The sky was clear, you could see only one star, which was almost a waste for that black immensity, in which many stars would reveal a memorable beauty and splendor.

He remembered that he was not alone and looked for the animal. When he looked, he had one more surprise: he was gone. His presence there had been as quick as that of the shooting star that tore the sky above his head as he searched for it.

He woke up taking a leap over the bed, if you can call it where he slept in bed. He still had in mind the huge blackened sky of the Andes. Without realizing it, he touched himself to see if he was really there and sighed with relief when he confirmed it. Inside the house, everything seemed normal. But that was the problem.

He removed the sock he had used as a bandage and looked for the wound he had suffered the night before, looked at the tear in his pants, but could not see the wound. He bent his trouser leg to the knee and he was still there. That part had not been a dream. I had bled a lot, because the mattress was stained with blood. A little confused, he looked at his watch to see what time it was . Again something was wrong! It was already dawn, for he could see the light coming in through the cracks in the door, but his watch said twenty-seven in the morning. He decided to look outside the house to see that.

He opened the door, the cold air outside the house found him again. The interior of the house had been very well heated by the few pieces of wood he had left burning in the fireplace. Houses built to withstand cold climates must have a good seal against the entry of cold air and consequently the exit of hot air. He looked out of the house, everything seemed to have changed. With the dawn everything had become more secure. Easier to face. What he really wanted at that moment was to be able to understand what had happened. But there was only one doubt: He didn't know if it had really happened or if he had dreamed.

Looking closer at the clock, he realized that it was not working properly, perhaps due to the fall. He decided to think about it later, as he had barely arrived and considered that it had been caused by the tiredness of the trip. Or maybe it could be something in your own mind. Your unconscious, perhaps? Or could it be somnambulist? Who would know?

He had agreed with his friend that during the time he was living in the house he would do minor renovations and take care of cleaning the surroundings. After a thorough observation throughout, she realized that she didn't have much work to do. The parts that needed to be renovated were: the two doors, which were slightly corroded by termites; the roof that had some broken tiles and the two windows that had broken glass. Outside the house, at the back, there was a place very similar to the underground hurricane shelters that existed on US farms. He assumed he would find some tools there to assist with the renovation.

As he prepared to open the door he noticed that it was, for the most part, scratched. As if something or animal had tried to open it. He was almost forgetting his supposed dream, at that moment the memories surfaced as if he were living that strange moment again. He took a deep breath and controlled himself, went back to thinking about the work he had to do, then he held the lock on the door very hard and pulled it. The door opened and dozens of rats came with it. He jumped to the side and dodged them, not so much out of fear, but to avoid contact. He stood beside the passage and watched them leave, calmly.

Until that moment, he was not able to judge any form of life, so he didn't even think about killing them. Looking at the rats, he started thinking about how good it must be to live, caring only for his own livelihood. The evolution that man went through, which many say is the factor that defined his stay on Earth until today, seems to have stalled the instant he was able to feel safe. What nobody could see is that the real evolution that man should go through is one that concerns his way of thinking and caring for his fellow man, regardless of the degree of kinship or affinity. The world is going through a very delicate phase, people motivated by personal gain, end up becoming more selfish every day. Seeing the world as a way to take advantage of yourself.

The rats were certainly there, sheltering from the cold, from the rains, breeding or perhaps even hiding from some possible predator, which would justify the scratches on the door. He had already wasted too much time, so he thought it best not to be imagining things anymore. He decided to search the supposed cellar. He would have to carefully clean up before that, the kind of service he didn't like very much. During the cleaning he came across some more mice, cockroaches, spiders and other insects of the type. In the small room, which was about two meters wide and one and a half deep, there were some things. Plates, pots, cutlery, glasses, some personal belongings of the former owner who was familiar to his friend. Or whoever had lived there before. Mostly worthless things.

There was also a small chest, similar to a jewelry box, only a little bigger. It was all worked and had many odd-looking carvings. It had two hinges on the back of the lid. A huge old lock on the front kept the box closed. He was a little afraid about it. Also after what happened the night before, it was not surprising that he was doubting everything around him. After a while he thought he was just letting his imagination run wild when he thought that in the trunk he would find something unexpected. It was certainly a tool chest, nothing more.

With that in mind, but still a little unsure, he took the trunk and took it outside the little room. There he was more enlightened and would have more freedom to work. He thought for a while to see how he would open the lock without having the key, it didn't take long to discover that he would have to break it. He went into the house and took out his hunting knife. I didn't think I could break that huge lock with that insignificant knife. It hit, but the sound of steel whizzing showed that it wasn't going to be easy. He looked around and found a stone. He held it in his hand and tapped it as hard as he could. The padlock did not break, but the ring attached to the box that held it and was much more corroded than it broke near the wood.

He took the knife and finished opening the part that had broken. He removed the padlock and thought for a while before deciding to lift the lid. Contrary to what he expected, he found no tool in the trunk. It was very dirty and at first it only saw a lot of dust. Passing his hand to remove the dust, he touched a solid part. And they certainly weren't the expected tools. When he realized what it was, he was surprised. It was a small book.

A very old looking little book. He took it and leafing through it realized that it had been written in a dialect that he was unaware of. It wasn't really a book, it was more like a pamphlet. I didn't know many dialects, but if it was a language I had seen before, I would certainly have recognized it. There were also some engravings on it. He knew very little about the history of South American natives. He imagined it was some account of the ancestors of the natives who inhabited the Cordillera.

As he flipped through the booklet, he went through something that caught his eye. It was a very old-looking print. The engraving was very similar to a statue, which is only found on Easter Island. Everything was very strange, because there were moments that it seemed to be dreaming and moments that the reality was frightening. How could those people know Easter Island and its details being so far from the American continent? The booklet had a cover of some kind of wood. A sunlit mountain was carved into it. He assumed that it should represent the mountains of the Cordillera. The leaves of the book were very old, so they were so dry that if they were folded they would break. They were well yellowed and very wrinkled, as if they had been assembled in a hurry, without much care.

I had to take great care to be able to leaf through without damaging it. Even though he was very old, he kept his few written words and pictures in very good condition, even appearing to have been made a few days ago. He saw many interesting things drawn on it. But there was something that differentiated that booklet from others, it seemed to maintain an order of events, seeming to describe some kind of story. A report or perhaps a diary.

He decided that he would not start working that day, because everything up to that moment had been very strange and his leg still hurt a little. He decided to investigate the things that were happening. He had to find something that would explain everything in a logical way, so that he could calm down and start renovating the cabin. He walked, and went around inspecting the house, looking at the ground and places where he had not been, but nothing seemed to be out of place. There were no footprints, nor scrubbed woods. Nothing that showed any strange events.

He looked around again. Then to the lake and the forest. Then to the mountains in the distance. He took a deep breath and filled his lungs until he almost burst, that air that came from the Cordillera was so refreshing and pure. Everything seemed to be calm and this was not pleasing to him. Thinking for a while, he decided that he would try to find out about the village he had passed through previously, which was about five miles away. The road was very winding and full of ups and downs. There were many stones covering the road, and these stones were large, which made walking on the road a very time-consuming feat. Besides, I knew it would be very difficult to get any information.

And if he told what really happened, or what he thought had happened, they would surely think he was a lunatic. But this was not just a dream. He sensed something about it. There was something behind those visions, hallucinations . Or whatever they were. Suddenly he started to hurry. He put the book he found in the trunk into his backpack. He left about five minutes later and, looking at his watch, noticed that it still wasn't working properly. Going back down the road, he realized that last night, when he got there, he hadn't noticed several things. Perhaps because of the rush to get there before nightfall.

He saw that the road stretched in a way that he could barely know whether the next turn was to the right or to the left. Winding with ups and downs hiding the parts that were ahead. Suddenly he felt a chill go through his body and looking back he seemed to see something hiding among the vegetation. His fear returned and quickened his pace. What if the road ended at any moment? What if you were dreaming again? What if he had died the night before and was a ghost who should have gone through it forever? Without realizing it, he started to walk even faster and, in a few seconds, his thoughts were again lost in fears and anguish. It seemed that someone or something was following him, looking everywhere for signs of this, but he could make no distinction. He tripped and almost came to the ground. He barely noticed the small drop. He was afraid and his only intention at that moment was to walk as fast as possible.

He looked at his watch and saw that it had been just over an hour since he left for the village. He was sweating a lot, despite the fresh air that covered the slopes he passed. By his calculations, he would arrive at the village around noon.

He heard the last night's growl again, but it seemed far away. Or was it your imagination? He looked back, because that was where he came from. Another shiver ran through his body. Another grunt was heard and this time it seemed to have come from very close. Whatever it was, it was on his trail and would reach him at any moment. He had three apparent options: The first, and least likely, was to stand there and see what was coming; The second was to hide and wait for everything to pass before moving on; The third, and most likely for him, was to start running. He was already very close to his goal and the movement of the village could frighten the animal that was chasing him.

He started running down the gravel road. The backpack on his back started to get in the way, causing him great discomfort. He held it in his hands and kept running. He ran as fast as he could for about five minutes, then slowed down and started walking again. He was breathless and hungry, because until that moment he had eaten nothing. He opened the backpack and got a snack, but he didn't have time to eat it. When he started to eat he heard the grunt again. This time much higher and much closer . He looked back, but it was too late: The animal was about fifty meters away, and was running towards him.

He threw the snack, as the animal could stop to eat it, so he would have more time to escape. He started running again. He no longer felt his legs, as he had made a great effort until that moment. He didn't have the courage to look back, nor did he have time for this. If he wavered just for an instant, he wouldn't know what could happen to him. He began to understand how prey felt when hunted. For a moment he thought he could escape, but gradually he began to hear the animal's breathing approaching. The puffs were becoming more real. He felt a breath of air coming from behind and he barely had time to feel the heavy weight fall on him and the darkness take over.

TWO

It was a very beautiful morning, from which the best things are expected. It was still early, and last night's dew covered the undergrowth around his house. As usual, she washed her hands and face, brushed her teeth, put on her white shirt, combed her hair and made a long braid. He took some things and left for the service. I didn't usually feed in the morning, even if a lot of people thought it was wrong. Even herself.

She passed by a few houses, always greeting people. They were mostly rural workers who were preparing for work. She was always moving on without stopping to talk. He was a very dear person in the village, as he had already done much more than he imagined for some of those people. He got to his job: the local medical post. That it was in a very old house, with the walls worn and without any painting, the windows and doors were of a very old time. The door was of the type that opened in the middle, with two leaves, and a lock that, when turned, unlocked it. He opened half the door, and looked briefly to see if everything was in order, wondering for a moment why it wouldn't be.

Nothing serious had happened there since he arrived, keeping everything under his control from the beginning. He opened the windows and sat down in his chair. Soon someone would arrive with some daily problem: hand strains, headaches, the flu, someone with a hangover . Nothing that would overcome the seriousness of this.

Victor lay on the road. Still half asleep, not knowing what had happened. I could only feel a huge pain coming from his back. I was dizzy and dizzy. Or are they visions? I heard people talking. His mind was spinning. And as much as he tried, he didn't even know, he remembered nothing that had happened after his fall. When he struggled to remember, his head felt like it was going to burst and the images swirling in the end ended up taking him back into the darkness.

The light falling on his eyes was unbearable. He sat on the bed, but did not recognize the location. He looked at his arm and saw needle marks. He saw some empty bottles lying on a table and assumed he was in a hospital. He struggled for a moment, sitting on the bed and putting his hand over his forehead, tried to remember something that had happened. His head spun again, so he had to lie down again. The moment the bed went to bed it made a huge creak. The bed was very well maintained, but from the creaking sound it also noticed that it was very old. Someone in the next room heard the noise he had made and came to meet him. He was a young boy, no more than fifteen years old. He assumed he was a nurse, as the boy was still too young to be a doctor.

The young man began to speak in Spanish, but realizing that Victor had little understanding of what he said, he motioned for him to wait and left. A few minutes after his departure, another person entered the room. And because of her way of acting, and her age, she was not a nurse. After checking the pulse and blood pressure, she spoke in Portuguese, but with a little accent:

- Good Morning! Are you feeling better sir? His voice was as soft as the mountain breeze, his dark hair was slightly curly and his eyes shone like black pearls. For a moment he forgot that he was in a hospital, but he soon recovered.

- It's all right. Thanks for asking. But where am I?

- You are in an advanced health post, in the village Viento Serrado.

- What happened with me? How did I get here? He put his hand over his head in a gesture of doubt.

- Some farmers returning for lunch from the fields met the Lord just over two kilometers from here, on the road that leads towards the mountain range. The Lord was passed out and dehydrated! With serious injuries to the back and legs. She paused for him to assimilate. What struck me as an attack by some wild animal. She saw his eyes change as he told her how he had been found. Seeing her dispersed gaze, she realized that she was thinking about something. His eyes scanned the room and stopped in an empty corner of the room, staying there for a few seconds. Seeming to have come to himself, he continued:

- How long have I been here? Gradually I came back to reality and therefore I needed to know everything that had happened. I had to clarify everything and return as soon as possible to the cabin or, if it was more serious, to Brazil.

- Well, the Lord . She barely started to speak and he interrupted her.

- Please don't call me sir anymore! My name is Victor, and despite the state I am in, I am only twenty-three years old. I don't consider myself the master of anything . he said, looking more relaxed.

- Okay, as you prefer Victor. But to answer your question: You have been in my care for two days. Realizing the impact that certain things she said caused him, he decided to be more discreet and not be so direct from that moment.

He was surprised, as he thought he had been there for an hour or two at most. He wanted to take action on all this, but his mind was very tired. Perhaps because I was going through situations I had no control over. Or worse, I didn't even understand them. He looked at the woman, who until that moment did not even know her name. He was about to ask one more question, but before he did she interrupted him:

- Don't say anything else, please. I will ask you to rest for a while, as it is still very weak. If you want we can continue to chat later. She turned to leave, but before it was out of reach, he took her hand and prevented her from leaving.

- Doctor, will you allow me one last question? She nodded her consent.

- What's your name? She was undecided. Thinking that until a few minutes ago he was asking about himself, looking very distressed. Suddenly his interest had changed. He thought that was strange, but he replied naturally:

- My name is Estela.

She looked at his hand and looked at him for a moment. In his eyes he could see a hint of pity, or discomfort, he was not sure. Maybe it was fear. She turned and left as quickly as she entered, leaving him with no further goodbyes. Victor, after a lapse in thinking, returned to reality and began to think about everything that had happened. I had to do a thorough review of everything that had happened, but I couldn't concentrate. Perhaps it was the effect of the drugs he was taking.

He thought again about the possibility of abandoning it all. Forget what had happened and go back to your peaceful life in Brazil. I had to analyze the possibilities very well, because I knew that if I made the wrong decision I would never forgive myself for that. On the other hand it could be exaggerating. Everything could be explained if a hungry wild animal was found nearby. At this time of year, food is scarce, and animals are forced to eat what first appears to them. Or it could also be some female protecting her young. But on second thought, this was unlikely: If she was protecting her offspring, she would not leave the place where they were, leaving them exposed to other predators.

Thinking a little more, he came to the conclusion that it was the greatest threat of that habitat. The human race had become the main responsible for animal deaths in the entire existence of our planet, apart from the possible impact of the meteor that would have caused the disappearance of dinosaurs and the flood of Noah. Two facts not yet unanimously accepted in society. Deep down the animals were right to try to defend themselves.

His daydreams were interrupted again by the nurse. He went in quietly, straightened his pillow and changed his pillowcase. He had a smile of curiosity. Victor was going to ask him something, but he thought it best not to try, because he might be wrong. But that was not like him. Never before had I been afraid of making mistakes! And it wouldn't be his first time. He asked the boy what his name was, but he looked at him curiously, and finally replied:

- You can speak in Portuguese, Dr. Estela taught me some things about your language.

- Oh how nice! This makes everything much easier! But where did she learn to speak Portuguese? Because to be able to teach you she must speak very well .

- Didn't she tell you? And seeing that the answer was negative, he continued. The doctor is Brazilian. I thought I already told you. Well, because you're from there. You are Brazilian, aren't you? He asked to confirm his expectations. But Victor was slow to answer, as he wondered why she hadn't told him that. It didn't really matter in the end, given the circumstances.

- Yes I'm brazilian. And not! She hadn't told me she was from there. Thanks for telling me. I am more comforted in knowing this. While they were talking, the young nurse was doing his job, without letting the conversation take away his concentration. He proved to be a very determined and hardworking boy.

- But as I already asked you in my terrible Spanish. What's your name?

- My name is Juan. The people in the village call me Juanito. What about you, what's your name?

- Mine is Victor, but everyone calls me Victor. When he finished speaking, he laughed, but saw that the boy had not understood, so he frowned again. He had never been good with jokes .

- You have a strange name! Who gave it that name? Isn't that a prince's name? Or a famous conqueror of ancient times?

Victor was silent, but made a gesture of thanks. That was a great compliment to him. Who would have thought? Being called a prince. He smiled to himself. He began to wonder if the fact of being isolated that whole day had not been the real reason for his daydreams. He looked for Juan again to ask other questions, but he was already gone. It didn't matter, he was already feeling much better, so he believed for a moment what he had just imagined. He decided to get up alone so he could look out the window. I wanted to see how everything was outside.

He managed to sit up in bed with great effort. This would be more difficult than I had thought. He took a deep breath and gathered the strength to get up. This time it was easier. He balanced a little, leaning against the wall. I was beginning to think that if I had to walk like this for the rest of my life, it might be better if I had died. But with a shake of his head the thought shook off. He continued straight towards the window.

Already in the window, his eyes searched for any movement they could detect, but nothing. The only thing he saw was a deserted street. He thought for a moment: A village that had a doctor should not be an abandoned village. He didn't feel his legs properly, but he started walking towards the door. Before he could reach her, the doctor surprised him by entering the room. The surprise left his legs unsteady, and as if they had disappeared he plummeted toward the floor. The woman ran towards him to lift him up and said in a whisper:

- Why did you get out of bed? His voice was strained and scolding.

- I was curious to see things outside the room. I thought it wouldn't hurt to have a look.

- You should know that lying a little more would be better. His wounds are still healing. As she spoke, she helped him back to bed.

- Well, you didn't say when you would come back, so . He thought for a while and ended up acknowledging that he had done wrong in getting up, and as she waited for a continuation he added: Well, I think you're right. I acted without thinking, but everything was over then . And before he could finish speaking she completed her sentence.

- So from now on you will follow my directions to the letter! He was amazed at her rigidity and defiantly replied.

- Yes, sir Captain! He gestured as if he were saluting. Then he laughed at himself and the disapproving face she made.

- Please stop your jokes! You have suffered very serious injuries to your legs and back, and I still don't know what caused it. His voice changed, and so did his voice. She realized that she had overreacted. Deep down he knew he had said too much.

For a moment, silence filled the room. They were dispersed in their own thoughts. Paralyzed looking at each other, but did not see each other.

Victor wondered if she could inform him of something that had happened, that would help him clear some doubts out of his head.

- I didn't want to disagree so quickly with you. I was just trying to forget reality a little. If what I am experiencing is reality. Victor said at last.

His eyes were heavy and he felt like crying. But it would not be so weak at this point. Not that I thought men didn't cry, on the contrary. If I cried at that moment, I would totally lose control. It would lose its bases and collapse. This was unacceptable! I still hadn't finished what started there. I didn't even know if it had started, but one thing was for sure: I wouldn't give up on my goal so quickly!

- Why don't you tell me what happened to you, maybe I can help you! Said the doctor.

- I don't know if what I'm living is really what I think it is, that's all, that's all. What can you tell me about the animals that live in the mountain range?

- In that regard, I can't help you much, because I'm a doctor, not a biologist. But regarding the animal that attacked it, I can make some observations if I really want to. Victor nodded for her to continue. Well, I've seen people who have been attacked by animals before and I found four basic differences between you and them: The first is that you were more attacked in the leg region. In the attacks I analyzed earlier, the victims had their abdominal region perforated, as it is a softer region and consequently requires less effort from the animal to pierce it; The second is that at this time this region is very full of food, which rules out the hypothesis that the animal was hungry. And wild animals only attack humans as a last resort, and often not even in these.

She paused, fixing something in the room.

- The third is that I never heard of an attack in that region, caused by a single animal, being as close as you were to the village and at the time when everything happened. Most animals usually attack at night and in packs, as they would have a greater chance of success.

When she stopped talking again, she thought for a moment about everything she had said, she started to imagine several answers that she could give to the other questions that arose in her mind .

- And lastly: For the first time, I'm talking to the victim, usually in such an attack, you can only find the body after a few days of having suffered the attack, which gives time for other predators to enjoy it as well. Which gives us a lot of work to identify the victim by the remains .

After that long, somewhat misleading explanation by Dr. Estela, he started to wonder why she had told him all that, in that way? Maybe I wanted to get you prepared for the worst? But what worse?

A thousand questions popped into his mind, looking at her he realized he was a little unsure maybe what he said. Maybe about how he had just acted. He thought that maybe she wanted to be knowledgeable about the subject, but deep down she also had doubts about what happened to him.

After telling him all that, he found no other way to calm him down than through sedatives. He knew it was temporary and this was his biggest fear. After I woke up, I would definitely come back to you with your questions and have no way to escape. He couldn't think about it anymore, so he decided to go home and get some rest. Then I would return to be on duty. He knew that if there was a problem, they would call her. He warned Juan about everything he thought was most important and, having nothing else to do there, went home to rest.

Juan, as was his custom, was packing up his medications. Suddenly a strong wind blew in through the window and carried along the small curtain, which in turn dropped the vials of medicine on the cupboard. Juan ran to close the window. Soon it would be dark and the night would be very cold, which was typical in that region. As he approached the window, he felt a strange shiver run through his body. The silence outside was deathly scary. It seemed that life had stopped. Nothing was making noise. Even the dogs were gone. They were always barking on the street, but they weren't there at the time.

He thought about what the ancients were saying about the boy and imagined that it was as if an unparalleled predator was lurking, just waiting for the right moment to launch his deadly attack. Juan was still thinking about something when his thought was interrupted by a grotesque howl from far away. Had he imagined that? Without realizing it, she started to shake and dropped what she was holding in her hands. Many things came to mind: What kind of creature would make such a sound? What if the ancients were really right? He couldn't stay close to Victor for another minute! The creature would not rest until it had what it wanted.

His headache was unbearable. He got up slowly until he was able to sit. Everything still seemed to be spinning. He knew that if he remained seated he would vomit. The smell of the infirmary in these cases is a great aggravating factor. He lay down again, but he had in mind that it was just for air. He tried to recognize something around him and gradually became aware of where he was. He was very tired and when he recognized where he was he was discouraged. He had barely woken up and was already down. He remembered everything the doctor had said to him, and that didn't seem like a good thing. He closed his eyes and took a deep breath.

The attempt was to regain some of his sanity. He slowly opened his eyes and was taken aback by the figure that was staring at him. His movement was one of revulsion and defense. He struggled with such force that he fell to the ground. Dr. Estela jumped back, protecting herself as well. She was afraid that he would attack her, but she soon saw that it was a movement caused by impulse and it would be nothing more than that. She approached slowly so she could talk to him, still lying on the floor.

- Take it easy, Victor! I'm the one here! She spoke softly. It's me, Dr. Estela! Do not be afraid! I'm here to help you! Do not you remember?

Slowly, as if he had doubts about whether it was real or not, Victor began to relax his defensive position. Her eyes finally met Dr's and she saw that they were full of tears. I just wasn't sure if it was tears of thanks or fear.

- Come on Victor, talk to me! I'm already here! If you were afraid of something you need not fear anymore . I will help you! Promise!

His words sounded like a magic key that was able to unlock any lock. He blinked, coming to himself. It was as if he wanted to speak but the words did not come out. She approached slowly and bent down, standing beside him.

- I . I'm . He couldn't speak properly. When he tried to speak, his eyes looked at the horizon. As if he were immersed in his thoughts in search of something rational to say.

- Victor, we're all worried. But there's no use in hiding there. We will! Give me your hand! I help you get up.

She held out her hand for him to hold, but he hesitated a little. After a sudden shake of the head, as if he wanted to chase away bad thoughts or bad memories. To her surprise, he stood up alone. The doctor looked at him with some astonishment. When their eyes met again she could see that

Victor was not the type to give up easily. His gaze showed the willpower to keep fighting, as long as the last hope existed.

- How nice to see you didn't give up! She told him smiling.

- Give up why? Is that? Anyone could have gone through what I went through! He said, seeming to disagree on the subject.

She was getting up and stopped to see what he was getting at with that argument. He, seeing the doubt in his eyes, tried to explain himself better.

- Good! What I mean is that anyone can be attacked by a wild animal. I was just kind of impressed to imagine that it would never happen to me.

She continued to pay attention as if she still didn't understand. He, somewhat awkwardly, looked for a new way to explain himself.

- I think that when you are aware that something can happen to you, be it as grotesque as you can imagine, the consequences of that are easier to accept.

He tried to help Dr. finish finishing the bed, which after that moment, in his view, was no longer his, since he was fully recovered. When he raised his arm he felt dizzy and in order not to fall he had to lean on the bed. Even supported he thought that if he didn't lie down he would pass out. At the first sign of a fall, Dr. was already at his side helping him to lie down on the bed. His arms were wrapped tightly around him, giving him the support he lacked. She just straightened it, turned to leave, but couldn't, as her hand was being held.

- Calm down, I'm just going to get you something to eat. You haven't eaten properly for a few days and we should take advantage of your improvement to remove this delay.

He took a deep breath, seeming to take courage and finally said:

- I would like to apologize, because I know I'm being stupid with you.

She shook her head, showing that she was not worried about it.

- I want to take the opportunity to thank you for everything you have done for me. I know that if it weren't for you, maybe I would be dead now.

When he finished saying that, he pulled his hand away and in a gesture of affection and thanks he gave a light kiss.

She was surprised and a little embarrassed. Her face was pink and her expression was sheepish, but she managed to recover quickly.

- No need to thank! I didn't do anything that any other doctor wouldn't do! Furthermore, you are still not fully recovered. Rest while I get you something to eat. He let go of her hand and let her out and settled on the bed, closing his eyes for a moment.

When he opened them, he was scared because he was no longer in the room. He was walking through the old village. People were dressed in multicolored, rustic and cold clothing. They did not seem to notice it. Suddenly they started to run. Following his eyes, he saw that they were passing by him as if they were playing some kind of game. But he soon realized that something was wrong: They were all native and that place didn't even have a trace of civilization . At least not in the way he knew it.

The houses were so low that you had to go down first to enter. Mostly made of stone but there were also some made of wood. Turning his gaze back, in the direction they were coming from, he could see something that gaped at him. A huge truncated pyramid at the top was at the bottom of the landscape, contrasting with the mountain range. At the very top, something caught his eye: The gleam of something golden, reflecting the sunlight. It was a golden one that he had never seen before.

He started walking towards the pyramid and came to a square, where in the center there was a place that looked like an altar. Countless people gathered around the altar. Against his will, as if floating, he approached and saw that the cause of this was a beautiful young woman not more than fourteen years old. She was being held before, what appeared to be, a very old priest. Several men passed and spoke to the priest. In a solemn and immobile position the priest heard what each man had to say, always doing what he understood with a small nod. There were four men in total. After the story was finished, the elder began to utter a few words. I couldn't hear what he was saying. Only the words that the crowd repeated after the priest stopped speaking were clear:

- Capac Hucha! Capac Hucha! Capac Hucha! Capac Hucha! They all said in chorus.

The girl had no reaction to the man's pronouncement, appearing to be under the influence of some narcotic. She looked very healthy, as if she had been cared for very well. He wore a very sumptuous outfit with details that seemed to have been made of gold. On his head he carried a reddish ornament of a size disproportionate to the rest of his clothing.

Taking advantage of his condition, the elder approached, standing behind the altar. With him were the four men. He said a few words, seeming to be heading for the mountain peaks around the place. He raised his hands towards the sun, which from the position he was in seemed to be noon. Everyone around who was watching what was going on bent down to bow.

The girl seemed to regain her lucidity for a second by pushing with her hands as they put a rope around her neck. Two of the men held his body on the altar and the other two started to spin the rope around the young woman's neck. Apparently, they didn't want her to get marks, because they didn't press too hard.

They left the rope on the edge so she couldn't breathe. When the air started to run out, she again became aware of what was happening, but it was too late. He struggled for less than two minutes and stopped in a sudden spasm. In the next moment an astonishing silence came over the place. Turning his eyes to the altar Victor can see the young woman. It was practically a child. Once beautiful and full of life, now dead on the altar.

Many of those present began to cry. He concluded that they were people who knew the girl. Suddenly one of the men who was with the priest looked familiar to him and stared in his direction. For a little while he seemed to have seen regret in his eyes, but in the next instant their expression changed from regret to astonishment. Unconsciously he whispered something almost imperceptible to the people around him. But he raised his voice and his words caused quite a stir among those present.

The other people followed his gaze and came across Victor. The priest who already had his back to the altar turned. When he saw what was happening he gave a cry, which seemed to be a battle cry, to which many men responded as if it were a command. Without wasting time, they ran towards Victor.

After witnessing what happened to the girl he assumed it was not a good idea to wait and see what would happen to him. He tried to run in the opposite direction to the pyramid. The screams of the men behind him were terrifying. He felt something go through his leg, but he didn't have time to look to see what hit him. At that moment, he was only sure of one thing: He was certain that he would die, and apparently in a worse way than the young woman, because he was aware of everything that was going on.

His eyes snapped open. His breathing was labored. He felt that his pulse was racing and his face was wet with sweat. The doctor was sitting beside her bed making a compress of water on her forehead to force the fever to subside. She realized that he wanted to say something and motioned for her not to speak. He looked out the window and noticed that it was already dark. He felt very tired, his mind was unable to settle on anything concrete. He took a deep breath and closed his eyes. He felt Dr.'s hand tightly hold his. At the same moment he opened his eyes.

He was feeling desolate and the warmth that Dr.'s hand was giving him at that moment made him feel that there was still a thread of hope. His face took on the sketched shape of a smile. His eyes stayed for a long time on a single point until sleep took him in her arms and took him again.

It was still dawn when he opened his eyes, waking up. It was strange, but he felt his energies almost completely recharged. Looking around, he noticed the presence of Dr. Estela. She was hunched over the foot of the bed. Giving little grumbles while dozing. Victor didn't move, as he could wake her up. Besides, he was even enjoying being there. The view was more rewarding and beautiful than the Andes with its snow-capped peaks.

They stayed there for over an hour. He looked at Dr. and laughed at her grumbles, thinking how everything was getting better. She woke up suddenly, startled on the bed and kind of breathless. After realizing that he was in the office, he seemed to calm down.

- How long have you been awake? He spoke in a sleepy voice while rubbing his eyes.

- I don't know for sure . She seemed embarrassed that he didn't wake her up.

- And why didn't you wake me up as soon as you came to?

- "I came back to me"? What do you mean "I came back to me"?

- You were unconscious for over eighteen hours! Saying nonsense about a girl and her death . Anyway, some seemingly fantastic things.

- Eighteen hours? All this? Did I mention a girl?

He made a gesture that confirmed he was confused by all this. He thought for a moment. He thought it best not to comment on the dream he had had. She remembered him well, but she might think he was going crazy. He decided to change the subject, as he thought that resuming all that again would be very tiring for both of them.

- Well. But apart from the bad news, isn't there anything new? She was surprised to hear the question he had asked her, as she thought she would be nervous when she knew how much she had slept.

- Things here are almost always repetitive and we usually have no surprises. It seems incredible, but everything here continues as I arrived. Just over four years ago.

- It's good that we're getting to know each other better! He said, wanting to appear unconcerned. Have you been here for almost five years? It's a good time! And I bet it has been well used . You must already know the most beautiful places that hide behind these numerous mountains that surround us, right?

- Not really. I do not have much time. My chores take up most of my day, and the rest that is left over does not make much.

- I do not believe! He's been here all this time and he still doesn't know anything about this place!

- It is not like that either. I know this town and some places around the region very well .

She stopped short and was silent. I was unsure whether to continue with that kind of conversation. She knew where it could take her. But before he could end the conversation he started talking again, interrupting his thoughts.

- When it gets better, I promise I'll come and get you for a walk. And there's no point in coming up with these excuses that you don't have time for being a very busy person. After all that you are doing for me this is the least I can do to repay.

- Come pick me up? But where are you going? Don't tell me you intend to go back to the cabin?

As she spoke he could see that there was something wrong with her words. Shortly afterwards he discovered what it was . fear! She was afraid of something!

- Do not be afraid. Before I go back there I will buy a hunting weapon. I do not intend to hunt the animal that did this to me, but if he harasses me again I will shoot him in the air to try to chase him away.

- Victor, there are some things you need to know. She felt a little uncomfortable about having to talk about it, but she took strength and continued. The descendants of the natives who live here say that you are in danger!

He was unsure whether or not Victor would accept what she told him.

- The ancients say that you are being hunted . And seeing a look of doubt on his face, he tried to clarify. They say you are a very old demon, endowed with the power of several wild animals . that for some reason is behind you.

For a moment Victor's expression remained doubtful, but soon afterwards he was overcome by an indisputable certainty and spoke.

- Well. I don't know what to tell you . I always believed, or at least tried to believe, in most of the things that people said to me. I grew up believing that giving value to native culture is a great sign of development and respect, not only for myself but also for others.

She was attentive to his words. Very surprised that he had that kind of reaction, because anyone else would find her a fanatic or something.

- Since I arrived at this place I have had strange sensations and dreams. It looks like I've been here .

She thought she was going to surprise him with what she was going to tell him, but in reality it was she who was more surprised at every moment.

- I think I should live everything that is meant for me. So I will stay and continue with what I came here to do. After I fully recover, of course.

She looked him right in the eye. From that moment on she would never see him in the same way as before. At that moment he saw the real person who was hiding behind that face. A strong person and not afraid to face whatever his destiny.

- Who knew, huh? You are a really determined person. But there are other things I also need to tell you about this animal.

- Ah, I was already forgetting. I said interrupting her. I never give up on the first difficulty that appears to me! I am very insistent. And I also never believe one hundred percent of what they tell me! I always draw some conclusions on my own.

She nodded, showing that she understood everything he had said to her.

- What do you think about having a coffee? So we can talk more freely.

His invitation ended with a wide smile, which made refusing impossible.

THREE

They were in the small kitchen of the infirmary drinking a nice coffee that had been prepared by Dr. She knew that it was not indicated that he drank coffee, but a little bit was not a problem if they managed to have a good conversation. But their plans were not working very well, because the conversation they were having was not very pleasant.

- But Dr. I don't think you should worry so much. What attacked me has, in my view, a great possibility of being a wild animal, not the supernatural creature that you are telling me to be.

She made a face of exhaustion, showing that she couldn't stand having to argue with him anymore.

- Well Victor, you already know my opinion on the subject. She spoke as if the topic was enough. And I will not try to convince a person who has already made his decision, as I know you did. I just think you shouldn't be making your decisions so quickly. Why don't you wait for things to cool down? It may be that some farmer finds a cougar attacking his breeding, this would be a good indicator.

- I think you are right. When he said that the expression on her face seemed to become more calm. But I have to consider the time factor. Again her face changed.

- Time factor? What are you talking about?

- Before I came here I made a deal with my friend, the owner of the house where I am. It consists of the following: in exchange for going unpaid, I must renovate the house. I'm already late, because with these strange things happening it was no wonder. She looked at him with an air that didn't matter at the moment. Dr., to be honest with you, I have a duty to at least try to keep my word .

He said that with the intention of animating his own ego. Maybe find a reason to continue. The doctor understood that well, so she didn't want to conflict with him anymore.

- Okay, Victor. Now what do you think about going back to the infirmary? It is already late and you should take a medicine to make your euphoria go down a bit. She said jokingly.

- But, Dr., we didn't even have time to talk properly. And I was enjoying our conversation.

- I think we can talk some more .

- Thank you. I was really in need of a little more relaxation. I think the real therapy that is working on me is these conversations that we have from time to time, Dr. They do me so well, you don't even know.

- I am happy to know that I am, in one way or another, helping you. I'm enjoying the conversation too. It's been so long since I spoke to a person from Brazil and this is making me very happy. I don't know if you understand me, it's that I've been here for so long, living for the sake of my profession that I had already forgotten how cool it is to have a relaxed conversation.

As she spoke Victor kept on paying attention and nodding whenever he understood what she meant.

- All this time living with these people opened my mind to certain things, which I had no idea existed and were not part of my world until that moment. But after so long here I think I ended up forgetting certain things about the world outside. Things that I believed were essential to my life and today I see are totally superficial. Worthless in real life.

- On the contrary. I think that, because you are living with these two realities, this made you a much more prepared person than any other.

- If so, I'll review my concepts. This is a living example of this that I just told you: imagine if you were not here, none of this would be happening and I would not know what you just said to me. That's why I'm enjoying this conversation so much, because I know I wouldn't have it with anyone else here in the village.

- I understand. You felt lonely, even with many people.

After Victor said that, the two of them were thinking for a moment. They were indifferent about what they were talking about. They did not insist on approvals, they were only sure that they were happy to be there. This was very good. Victor was suddenly coming back to reality. He inhaled a great deal of air, perhaps with the intention of absorbing all the good that that moment had brought him.

- When I get better, which shouldn't take long, I go to a bigger city to buy a shotgun to take to the cabin.

Estela was still immersed in her thoughts. When she became aware of what he had said, she panicked the daydreams and returned to reality.

- I don't think it's a good idea. Besides doing nothing. If any forest authority finds you with an illegal firearm, you are a foreigner. I think you will have to make up a very good story.

- I will not change my mind about this Dr. I have my own beliefs about these things, and you already know almost all of them. I have to do what I think is right, I'm sorry if I go over the things that you believe. I've thought about this decision a lot and I wouldn't want you to be upset with me for making it. I want to have you as a friend.

She still didn't agree, but she knew she wouldn't be able to change his mind. At that moment, he thought it best not to insist, so he nodded.

- That's right Victor. So be it as you wish. But let it be clear that you will not leave here until you are completely recovered. Understood? She spoke seriously, but soon saw that it was not necessary, so she smiled trying to be relaxed.

- Yes Dr. I understand your concern perfectly. I know I am not an example of a patient . She grinned and added:

- Wow! You are getting worse and worse . This type of confession is a strong indication of this. It's time for you to go to bed!

Victor was going to say something, but before he spoke she raised her hand in a gesture of authority, preventing him from speaking. He didn't like the imposition at all, but he stopped himself. The two packed up, then headed for the room where Victor was supposed to sleep. She prepared an injection with some painkillers and went towards him.

- If I'm right this will be the last.

- I hope you are because I don't like injections very much, especially when they are to be applied to me.

- So that means we found Mr. Victor's weak point. She said in a playful tone.

- This is not a weakness. It's just that I get a little nervous because of the expectation of the pain. Not for the pain, but for your expectation .

Without him noticing, she quickly inserted the needle into his arm and started to inject the liquid. When Victor realized that he had already received all the contents, she removed the needle from his arm. It had been so fast that there was no time to feel pain. He felt more relieved by this.

- Juan will come in a few minutes to see if everything is fine with you. Good night!

She was already getting ready to leave when he took her hand again and said:

- Thanks again Dr. I don't know what would become of me if it weren't for Mrs. Thank you! Sincerely. His look showed a lot of sincerity and emotion.

She nodded that no thanks were needed. And after a last general look he turned and left. Minutes later, the young man with whom he had spoken earlier entered the door. His expression was tired.

- How are you? Asked Victor, making conversation.

- I'm fine sir, and I see that it has also improved . He was looking at him in a strange way.

- How are you? You look tired.

- Actually, I was thinking about what you said the night you were worse.

- Ah. Did you hear something? What I said? He was curious.

Juan was in doubt if he should talk to him about the matter, since Dr. had already told him not to speak to him unnecessarily. But he did not resist.

- Capac Hucha! You said.

- And does it mean something to you? Victor asked feeling a shiver run through his body at the words.

- The translation in your language is something like "Duty Splendid". But it is a very old ritual from my ancestors. In it the most beautiful children from the most diverse parts of the Empire were taken to the capital where they were recognized by the great oracle and returned with the duty to be prepared and, after a while, to serve as an offering to the local deities. They had to be the most perfect of all, because only then would they be accepted by the deities. It was not always done, only in times of transition of the Emperor and in special festivities such as Inti Raymi, which is still celebrated by many today.

- What are you telling me? Do they still sacrifice children today?

- No! Please don't misunderstand! This hideous rite has not been performed for more than five hundred years. The fact is that almost no one outside our community is aware of it. That's why I thought it was strange that you mentioned it while you were delirious with a fever.

And thinking that he had said too much, the boy left without saying goodbye, leaving what he was doing in half. Victor called to him, but it was too late. He was confused again and started to recap everything they had talked about that day. Tiredness was slowly taking him to sleep and it didn't take long for it to go out.

He woke up with the impression that he was going to fall off the bed, holding the bed guards firmly. I wasn't sure what I felt, just sure that I was afraid of something. Looking around, he immediately recognized where he was. He took a deep breath and pinched himself to make sure he was awake. Looking around him in detail, he realized that he was alone, and that it must be too soon. A faint ray of light came in through a crack in the window. He got up and walked towards the window.

He opened the lock and pushed one side of the window out. As soon as it opened, you could feel the cold morning air coming in and touching your still-warm face. Their perspectives seemed to be right. The day had just dawned and there were residents on the street. When they saw that he was at the window, everyone was silent and started walking quickly. They entered the houses, then locked the doors. When he was beginning to worry about the silence and loneliness that the street was once again, he looked down the street and saw a person coming quickly in that direction. She was dark-skinned, with fair skin, and had curly black hair. His walk was quick and decisive. It was Dr. who was quickly approaching the office and apparently she was not very happy with anything.

- Victor, what are you doing there at the window? Did you know it can get worse if you take this direct cold air? She was apparently worried about him, or the comments of the natives, who knows .

- I'm sorry Dr. I didn't know that a glance out the window would be so disastrous. She realized that something had worried him.

- What happened before I arrived?

- There were some people on the street and suddenly when they saw me they stopped everything they were doing and hid inside their houses. I found that very strange.

"Didn't I tell you that the people in the village think you're cursed?" That's why they hid from you .

- Let's change the subject a little, I barely woke up and we are already in this conversation again. When do you think I'll be discharged?

- I don't know for sure, but it seems to me you could already leave the clinic. From a clinical point of view you are cured. She paused, wondering if she would complete the sentence. Finally he said . But from a personal point of view I'm not sure.

- Please, Dr., we will not start over with the sermon. Since you think I can leave today, I need to schedule my trip to the city to buy the gun. Estela's face twisted when she heard that.

- What? Won't you tell me you haven't given up on this ridiculous idea of buying a gun yet? You seem like a very intelligent man, you should hear the voice of reason. Seeing that Victor's expression was one of indifference, she decided to stop there.

- I'm sad to have to disagree with you again, but as I told you, I must do what I think is right.

Hearing this Estela felt distressed, but decided not to show what she was feeling. A long silence took over the clinic for a long time. Both were thinking of starting a conversation, but neither wanted to start, finally Victor said:

- Since I can leave, I think I'll pack my things. I need to go as soon as possible!

- Okay. I am going to help you. His face was sad and deep down he looked like he was losing him forever.

- No need to worry, Dr. Just show me where my things are and I'll pick them up myself. I don't want to take more work than I already did.

Then she took him to where his clothes had been stored and helped him pick them up. He noticed his sad face and decided to speak.

- We don't need to act like this is the last time we'll see each other! Why are we acting this way? This will not be our last meeting, I promise you! Don't you remember that I promised to take you to see the most beautiful places in these mountains?

- I don't know if I can go . I said with disdain.

 Victor made a face that would accept no excuse, and she recanted.

- Maybe I can find an empty schedule. I said I was sure I would never see him again.

- Very well, Dr. When I get back, I'll stop by and mark the day of our tour, okay?

- Of course yes.

- I must leave then. The bus will leave in a few minutes and if I miss it I will only be able to go tomorrow, and that is not what I want. Then, until the return, Dr. He said putting the backpack on his back and walking still limping.

- See you back Victor. But I want you to promise me something before I leave. And he looked at her curiously. When you get back I don't want you to call me Dr. or Mrs. anymore because I already got sick of hearing you say these pronouns all the time. Besides, we are no longer a doctor and a patient. We're friends.

- As you wish, Dr. She looked at him reproachfully, but he completed. Estela is only after I return, don't you remember?

He laughed and turned, leaving for the bus that left at seven sharp. She looked at him with the feeling that he would never come back. Deep down, maybe he hoped he wouldn't come back. If he came back he had no idea what he would have to face. Not even her .

He got on the bus, but soon realized that this trip would be totally different from the coming. The people on the bus were making room for him to pass. No one looked him in the eye, let alone addressed him. Some people were talking to the driver, apparently to try to convince him that he shouldn't take Victor. The driver looked at Victor's direction and gave a negative signal to people. He didn't know what it meant. But he soon realized that it meant he wouldn't get him off the bus.

When the news spread over the bus, many went down indignantly and headed for their homes. The few who were left were so tired that they barely noticed when the bus started to move. The bus maneuvered at the end of the street and continued to raise dust on the dirt road that led to the nearest city. Victor was a little sad to have to leave so quickly, but he consoled himself because he knew he would be back soon.

Estela was packing up at the clinic, but she couldn't help thinking about Victor. He saw that his job was not going to go well, as he barely knew what he was doing there. He left what he was holding on top of an old wooden cupboard and headed for the kitchen. I felt an uncontrollable need for coffee. He sat down and picked up the bottle, but it was empty. She was outraged by her bad luck. I didn't want to make coffee, I just wanted to drink it. It took a while, but he took a deep breath and took the energy to do it.

When he finished putting the water on the fire, a person came running through the clinic door talking quickly. She turned off the fire and went towards the lady who entered. She was an old woman, well known to Estela. Seeing that she was confused and nervous, he asked her to calm down and spoke calmly:

- Calm down, Assumption! What is happening? The woman was very nervous and could barely speak.

- It's Juan Dra. He's very strange! Very strange.

- Tell me what he has.

- He was also cursed . The animal stole my son's soul. Please help me.

After hearing that Estela was very nervous and ran to get her things. I had to go see Juan as soon as possible.

- We will! We can't wait. Said Estela, taking some things that she might need.

The two went out towards Juan's house. It was a very humble house, built of stones and wood, both found in that region. Elevations caused by stones that had not been covered by the mortar made of clay could clearly be seen at certain points on the wall. Juan was lying on a wooden bed covered with straw and with a very thin foam mattress on top.

She approached the bed to get a better look at her patient and was startled by Juan's appearance. He was pale and with dark circles almost black, he looked like an undead. He hesitated for a moment, for he felt a little dread. But when she looked directly at him, she realized that whoever was there was her friend Juan, the nurse's apprentice who helped her so much. His heart was filled with an intense feeling of sadness and anguish.

She approached him and took his hand to try to give him confidence. Her hand was cold and immediately she asked her mother to bring something to warm him up. While the woman left, Dr. approached him, hugged him and spoke in his ear:

- I'll take care of you, Juan! You don't have to be afraid anymore. I will do everything to make you better.

His gaze remained unmoved, but his countenance seemed to calm. The woman arrived shortly afterwards, bringing more blankets.

- It won't be enough! He needs an external heat source, like fire, or something.

- Okay doctor, I'll look for something.

Again the woman hurriedly left. The doctor then discovered Juan's top and opened his shirt. Then he opened his briefcase and pulled out a stethoscope. He began to examine his breathing and heartbeat. The two appeared to be normal. Your next step would be to ask your mother to make you a calming tea. Maybe if you slept a little and were just impressed with all those events, you would come to. He got up to see if the lady was returning. The moment Juan realized he seemed to come to himself and spoke desperately:

- Don't leave me, doctor! I am afraid that the demon will come in search of my body. Last night he saw me and I know he will come after me . He was panting and his eyes showed great dread.

Realizing that he was much more nervous than she imagined, she thought it best to give him an artificial tranquilizer.

- Calm down, Juan! I'll just get you some medicine.

She quickly left for the infirmary. He took the medicine and returned. On the way, some people were curious about the doctor's haste and followed her to Juan's house. Her mother was waiting for her with four hot stones. She told them to wrap them in cloths and place them under their feet, and just above their heads. She gave him the tranquilizer, and snuggled him under the covers his mother had brought.

It was not long before he fell asleep. Estela stayed by his side for another hour. Gradually he seemed to return to normal. She still wasn't sure what had hurt him. But the people who were outside the house already. And this was not good .

Victor had already been sitting on that bus for about forty-five minutes and couldn't take the discomfort any longer. His feet and hands were freezing. His wound hurt. He tried to get some sleep, but there were so many bumps that he could barely start to doze off. When he did, he soon woke up scared by the crashes that came from the suspension of the bus. If he still had suspension.

It was almost ten when the bus arrived in the city. He got off slowly, always being watched by everyone on the bus. Normally someone else would come down there, as it was the center of the city. But that day everyone seemed to prefer to go down a point or two further on. He had barely got off and the driver had already started the bus in motion, almost causing an accident. Maybe hoping to never find him again.

The problems had only just begun and he knew it well. He took his little Portuguese-Spanish dictionary and started looking for a hunting store, camping, in short, any place where he could find a gun or get references on where to find it. He walked in many places, but in all they said the same thing to him, looking at him with an air of suspicion.

I would never be able to buy a firearm as a foreigner and with a sawn mark made by the local police. A little discouraged and a little hungry, he decided to eat something, as it was almost lunchtime. He entered the first place he found. It was a heavy bar. I was going to take the opportunity to see if I could get any information about the weapon. He sat down on a stool outside the counter. When placing his order the man who served him noticed his difficulty in Spanish and was immediately saying:

- I speak a little Portuguese, sir. Ask me to try to see what I can do.

- I would like to eat something. But first I wanted to see if you can give me information. The man nodded, showing that he understood. Can you tell me where I can buy a hunting weapon? The man did not seem to understand or was in doubt whether he understood correctly. With a gesture Victor left no doubt about his intentions. A shotgun, revolver, or anything like that . he said, gesturing.

He understood, and made a surprised face at the fact that Victor had barely just sat down and broached such a subject.

- What will you want to eat? He said as if he was not giving much importance to his previous questioning.

Victor pointed to something exposed on the counter and the man took it.

- And to drink?

- It could be a soda. He said hopelessly.

The man served him and motioned for Victor to wait. He went towards the back of the establishment that had exposed walls and was worse than the "saloons" of the old American west. It was a smelly place. The floor didn't seem to have been cleaned in over a year. There were a few tables spread over a small area at the bottom of the place.

The boy who had served him was heading for that part of the bar. Some people were sitting there. All of them look bad. Victor worried a little, as the boy might not have liked the way he had harassed him. Or thought he was some kind and threat or a policeman. He thought it best to wait for the boy to return and tell him that he had been confused and that he was not what he wanted.

- Better to talk and get out of here. He thought.

The man had been talking to someone for some time and now and then they looked in Victor's direction. Suddenly the boy came back and said:

- We don't do this kind of business here! He said, ending the matter. And when Victor was getting ready to talk, he completed. But there is a person at the bottom who can help you.

Saying this he pointed to an old, tall man who wore a hat resembling a beret that the military wears.

- Thanks for everything. One more coffee, please! After picking up the coffee, Victor headed towards the man who apparently was waiting for him.

The two nodded to each other, then Victor, a little embarrassed to be on his feet, pulled up a chair and sat down.

- The guy at the counter told me that you can help me get something I'm looking for. He said in Portuguese, as he thought it best to be cautious this time, so as not to fall into any trouble.

- Yes, I have some equipment that may interest you. While talking the man lit a cigarette and inhaled deeply.

- And . These equipments do not come with any surprises, do they?

- Of course not, I am a person who takes what I do seriously. Imagine, I have to maintain my reputation . or other customers will never appear again. Do you agree? And he burst out laughing hard until he ran out of air and started coughing.

"This guy must have a Marketing expert helping to promote him." Weighed Victor.

- Of course I agree. But I need to know what their prices are, to know if I can pay for the equipment .

- Hey. Take it easy, man! Every thing in its own time. And he paused to cough. Have you ever bought something like this?

- Not really. But it shouldn't be too difficult. Is not it?

- Well, you're actually right. The most difficult thing is to find someone who can supply you, and this you already have. What kind of equipment are you looking for?

- I have a cabin in the mountains. Some animals are pestering me and my creations. I don't want anything special or modern. Victor found it unnecessary to speak the truth, as there would be many questions about the animal, which could even arouse the curiosity of local hunters.

- I'm not interested in the story of your life. Said the man dryly. But luckily, you came to the right guy. I have some old rifles, but in perfect condition that I think you will like.

- Actually, I didn't intend to hurt the animal, but only to scare it. So I'm looking for something that makes more noise than damage . If you know what I mean .

- More noise? Let me think . Everything I have makes a lot of noise. And also a lot of damage, when you hit the target . They're old and don't have any extra hunting equipment. Aside from that, I have nothing else.

- How much would one of these go with twenty projectiles?

- I'll make you a nice price, because I like you. I want two hundred and fifty dollars for the set. Just convert to "pesos de las leies" and bring me.

- Thank God you liked me! Victor spoke ironically, where the man closed his smile. It's kind of expensive, but I'm not really aware of the price of this type of thing. I don't have all this money with me and I will need to go to the bank to make a withdrawal. How long does it take you to get the gun?

- Are you in a hurry?

- Yes I am! I have to take the bus back to my ranch at five in the afternoon. Otherwise, I won't be able to go there until tomorrow. And this is not my intention!

- Right then. I'll be back here in an hour and a half. Is it good for you?

- Great.

After saying that, the man gave him a confirmation signal, got up and left. He followed the street until he entered an alley. Victor left too, but his destination was different. He was worried for a while. He thought he might be being followed and then being mugged. He quickly reached the city center and had no trouble finding a bank. Since he brought traveler's checks, he could withdraw money almost anywhere he owned a bank.

The operation was over quickly and as it was still very early he decided to have a decent coffee, because the one in the bar was horrible. He found a large market and took the opportunity to buy some things he might need while he was at the cabin. Starting to think a little, he thought it best to stop by a pharmacy and a gift shop. He had to buy a first aid bag, some medicines and a gift for Estela who had helped him a lot.

When he finished his shopping it was past three in the afternoon, and he only had half an hour to get to the treated place. It didn't take long to get there. The city did not offer many traffic difficulties, as it was very small and he was on foot.

When she got to the bar she couldn't find the man she had dealt with. He thought it was natural, as it was still ten minutes before the deadline he had given. He ordered another coffee just to be able to sit and wait.

Impatient to have to wait for the man who should be arriving at any moment. He was very impatient and thought that people noticed. He got up and headed for the door.

Looking through the door of the bar in both directions, he could not see anyone who looked like that guy. The street started near a small round plaza with a waterless fountain in the center. You could see the clear disdain people had for her. There was nothing in it: not even trees; nor grass; or even a bank, . The street continued among some houses that were already discolored by time and others in cladding, with exposed bricks. Moving on, he passed the bar he was in and headed straight west.

He looked at his watch and saw that it was five minutes past the deadline given to him by the man. He crossed the bar again to deliver the cup and pay for the coffee. Shortly after paying, the man at the counter said:

- You seem to be waiting for someone. Can I know who it is?

- I'm waiting for that man I spoke to this morning. He should already be here with something I ordered from him.

- May I know what you asked of him? The man was being too curious and this caught Victor's attention.

- Well. He looked around to make sure the boy who had spoken to him in the morning was not around. I asked him to get me a hunting knife. He lied because he didn't want to have any problems with the man.

The man looked at him with an unconvinced look and turned his back to Victor, saying:

- I think you're lying. And if what I think is true, you will have big problems here!

Victor started to get scared and before the man realized, he replied:

- I don't know why you're worried. Whatever I'm consuming, I'm paying for. And my private business is not about you! He spoke like that to test the man and see if he would stop pushing him.

Amazed by Victor's reaction, he immediately stopped what he was doing and, with a little anger at what he had said, replied:

- From the moment you come to do business inside my bar, I have every right to know what it is about! Do not you think?

Deep down he was right, but he would not correct what he said at that moment. He apologized and left the establishment. He went to the corner and waited for the man there. Twelve minutes later, when he was about to give up and leave, the guy surprised him, coming from behind.

- What are you doing out here? He asked visibly nervous.

- The boy from the bar was asking a lot of questions so I decided to wait here .

- We can't do this here in the middle of the street! Follow me that I know a place to end this .

The two walked down the sidewalk until they reached an alley in the middle of the block. They stopped next to a large trash can. On an old wooden crate the man bent down and placed the package. He unrolled it so he could see what he was buying.

It looked like a rifle I'd seen on television, but I wasn't sure. He looked a little old, but that was what he would get from an illegal purchase. The man showed him how to load the gun and gave him four more projectiles than he had asked for, as the magazine was for eight shots. Victor held the gun that weighed no more than five kilos. On the back was an inscription that caught his eye: "U.S. Rifle - M1 Garand - WW2 ". He had no idea what they meant, but he found it curious.

He gave a quick overview. He wasn't a weapons expert, he just wanted to make sure he wasn't spending money on something that wouldn't serve the purposes he envisioned. Satisfied with what he had seen, he wrapped the shotgun again and took out the amount he had previously agreed with the man.

- Here's your money. He said, handing a small wad of bills to the man.

- Be careful when using the gun to avoid problems. Said the man as he quickly counted the money.

While Victor was preparing an evasive response, the guy turned his back and left, putting his money in his pocket and crossing across the street. Victor, seeing the man's indifference, tried to act the same way. He put the bundle in his backpack so it was less apparent and started walking towards the bus stop that would take him back to the village.

He walked for about fifteen minutes, reaching a huge square. This one was very different from the previous one and noticed people selling handicrafts in the center. As he still had a few minutes to go before the bus left, he went to kill his curiosity and see if he could find anything for Estela. Craft vendors had their products displayed on rugs placed on the floor around the monument in the center.

For an instant he seemed bewitched by the rocky monument in the center. He already seemed to know that from somewhere. But it was impossible, I had never been in that city before and I couldn't imagine where I could get to know it. In the end, maybe it was just an impression. One of the vendors who were there approached. Initially smiling he looked at him and seemed to look at him curiously, changing his smile to a more serious babble.

- Illa tiki, ricsillayman! Illa tiki, yachallayman! He said in a whisper.

Victor was surprised by the man's so direct harassment that he was now holding his arm. Usually people were a little afraid to approach strangers looking like foreigners in those cities. The biggest surprise was when the man removed his own necklace and handed it over, seeming to bow to Victor.

- No thank you very much! Said Victor, but the man didn't seem to mind and remained standing in front of him. Please, my lord, I don't want to buy anything. He insisted, showing he was broke.

To which the old man replied with a gesture that he was not selling the necklace but giving it the same as a gift.

- Please, sir, I can't accept it! I'm about to take the bus . And seeing that the man would not leave his sight until he picked up the necklace, he took it.

The man then bowed his thanks for his acceptance and stood in front of him without looking directly at him, his head slightly bowed in a sign of respect. Victor was at a loss as to what to do and looking around he noticed that other people also behaved like the old man. Feeling very embarrassed by what happened, he realized that if he stayed longer there, he would surely miss the bus.

Holding his backpack firmly, he placed the necklace he had won inside his jacket pocket and quickly left in the direction of the place where he would then embark back to the village. As he walked the man who had given him the necklace said to himself, as in a prayer:

- Tona Apac! Tona Apac! Tona Apac! .

Less than five minutes later Victor got on the bus, still stunned by it all. The aversion of people in the vehicle was evident. Everyone knew what had happened during their stay in the village and believed that his presence was a sign of bad luck.

In a normal situation, he would feel uncomfortable because he hated having the sensation of causing discomfort to other people. But at that moment, he was far from feeling that way. He found himself in another world, immersed in thoughts that not even he understood. He sat down in the first empty spot he found and a few shakes later he was already asleep. A deep sleep, very different from the coming trip.

FOUR

His eyes burned as he contemplated the sun that shone as if it were midday. He was lying on something soft, his head arched back. The light bothered him. He turned his head and saw that he was on a beach. The taste of salt water still irritated his throat and left no doubt that he had drunk a good deal of it. I just needed to sit for a while and think to find out what had happened. He sat down and immediately felt so dizzy at the end that he couldn't stand it and felt something rise in his throat, vomiting. He felt an acidic taste burning all over his throat and assumed it was because of the salt water he had ingested.

- Very well! Now I must improve.

And he barely thought about it, and another spasm of vomit, now bitter in taste and yellow in color, spurted from his stomach.

- What the hell! Thought. I must be really bad!

He took a handful of sand and looked for a moment. It was very white and different from what I had seen so far. He stood up and with his right hand flat on his forehead, he protected his eyes from the light while trying to find himself. His head was hammering with pain. I had never been in a place as strange as this. The heat was unbearable. The techniques of location by the stars he knew as a sailor were useless. He would have to wait until nightfall to be sure of his position.

He observed the position where the sun was likely to set. He found that the mainland was on the opposite side of the sunset. Since he didn't have many options, he decided to explore near the beach to see if he could find someone to tell him where he was. Suddenly, as if at a glance, he saw flashes of people shouting, the loud sound of thunderstorms, a frantic sway, gusts of wind. He shook his head in order to ward off the visions. They left, but together with their departure came another wave of nausea and vomited again.

He recovered and began exploring the area. He checked his personal condition and realized that he was not dressed properly for an exploration in that location. The intense heat and the forest that appeared after the sands asked for something different than usual. He took off his white tunic and wrapped it around his waist to resemble a swim trunks. He kept his sandals at his feet and his shirt thin, heading for a clearing that led to the woods.

Approaching the entrance he noticed that the trees were not very high and that the land had a marked presence of dark rocks. He decided to take the easy route he could find. The climb was very steep and if you ventured through more difficult places you could get hurt and even die right there. Attempted also to walk by places where you could have a good field of vision around. I didn't want to have surprises with wild animals. Only at that moment did he notice that he didn't even have a knife. If he were harassed by any threat, he would be easy prey.

He saw a small tree fallen in front of him. She had a regular torso and decided to use her torso as a defense until she found anything better. He took a sharp stone that he found on the ground and with the help of a slightly larger one, hammered the base of the tree until it could not stand and broke. In the same way, it cut the upper tip which was thinner and offered no resistance. Using the smaller stone he scraped the dry bark that was left on the tree. A few minutes later he had an efficient form of defense: a stick about two meters long and a good weight. From his point of view, that was enough for the moment.

The forest was not the most dense he had seen, but he could be lost if he did not pay attention. He walked up the slope for a long time. He estimated that he walked about six kilometers long. During the climb, he thought that when he reached the top, he would be able to see farther and thus be better located. The forest was full of life, little monkeys in the trees, different types of birds, with the most varied colors. He was ecstatic: I had never seen birds of those colors and shades before. They flew in large flocks and as they passed they made a tremendous noise. It was both beautiful and dangerous.

There were also several types of trees and plants of great exuberance. Its leaves were wide and long, a little different from what he had in his memory. The temperature below the pantry was very mild, but it didn't even match the low temperatures I was used to. At this point the sound of a waterfall caught his attention. He walked towards the sound, as he was very thirsty and did not know when he would find water again. The place where the waterfall was found was not very big. There was a small portion of standing water just below the drop, forming a shallow reservoir. He quenched his thirst by drinking large portions of the water.

He looked around and up, trying to see the sun. He didn't find it, but he assumed it was just over three hours before nightfall. As there was water there, he decided to look for a place nearby where he could take shelter. He decided to spend the night in the surroundings. Walking a little he found two rocks of medium height side by side one another. The distance between them was ideal for lying down and taking shelter. He decided that he would make a covering of wood, leaves and rocks over the crack. That way you could protect yourself from the night dew and rain, if they came.

He climbed medium-sized trees and removed some dry branches that he still found next to the main stem, but already dead. He placed them across the gap, leaving as little space as possible between them. He covered them with a type of large, wide leaf that he had found on a tree of a species he did not know. The trunk was very light and of low resistance. Above the leaves he deposited some small stones that he had collected on the surrounding ground. He believed that with their weight the leaves would not fly from there. Above all this he placed a thin layer of soil, thus managing to build a well-sealed roof of what could be his home for some time.

With other, thicker branches he began to close the back and front of the crack. He needed something to tie or tie the woods. He found a kind of branch with thorns that had good resistance and would do. He found them climbing trees, but he had to be careful when handling them, as they could not stand the fold and broke. He braided some of them thinner and saw that his resistance improved a lot. He used these braids to secure the fences he would use in the cracks. One was permanently fixed, as there was no need to move it from there. While the other was left on the floor, functioning as a portcullis. Where its base was attached to the floor by a loose braid and its top should be tied at night to the crevice ceiling, next to the woods that formed it supported it.

He took advantage of the kindling that came with the main woods and made a small stock of wood for the fire. He started to feel hungry and knew that soon he would have to get his food in some way. He would probably have to hunt and kill an animal for food and certainly not eat it raw. I would need to bake it, hence one of the needs of the fire. The other was that at night it could get too cold and would have to be heated somehow, if the fire was already lit it could heat some stones and take them into the crack and get warm. Another important factor was that most animals fear fire. Which would keep him safe for the night while he slept.

He looked for very dry grass and fine dry sticks to start the fire. Soon he found what he needed. He handled the materials with such skill that in a few moments a small smoke started to come out of the sticks. It was increasing and increasing. Until, as if by magic, a flame ignited. The moment he saw the small flame he was already prepared with more dry grass and deposited it on the small fire. A little more fine twigs and I was sure it wouldn't go out. Shortly before, he had already prepared a place on the ground for the fire. It was a small circle with some degree of unevenness around the ground. He made his outline with small stones so that the fire would not spread. He set the sticks on fire there and deposited some larger pieces of wood and more dry grass on them. The fire was ready!

His concern now referred only to food. What would you eat? He decided to make a trap similar to a bird-hunting cage and leave it set for the night. It was close to dusk and, hopefully, the next day I should have taken something. And that is what he did: he twisted thin branches of wood so that they were shaped like a pyramid. He set the trap a good distance from the camp. On the way from the camp to where he was he found some fruits and the remains of what he ate he used as bait, along with some flowers. Some of these fruits were in the high parts of the trees and were already pecked, so he believed they would attract birds.

There was no more time, it was starting to get dark and he could get lost because he still doesn't know the place well. He decided to leave everything for the next day and retire. Another thing that worried him was that most predators had nocturnal hunting habits. And I didn't want to be easy prey for any of them. He headed quickly for the crack. He went in, closed the wooden door and lay down. Before preparing the trap, he had cleaned the floor and fixed it by removing its undulations. He deposited a thin layer of dry grass on the ground. For his first night in that unknown place he was well prepared. He checked the lashing on the door. He lay down and put his staff aside. He was attentive to the noises that, from time to time, caught his attention. He heard nothing but the natural sound of insects and the gentle wind blowing in the treetops., Which encouraged him to sleep.

He opened his eyes quickly, lying motionless. The cry that woke him could still be heard echoing across the valley.

- What a strange dream! He thought and moved his eyes around.

I was scared and in doubt. It took a while to recognize where he was. When he remembered where he was, he took a deep breath and checked that everything was normal. The moon was in the crescent phase and the luminosity it provided was enough to see itself reasonably even in the middle of the night. He sat down, looking at the fire and saw that only a few small embers remained in its central part. He opened the door carefully and picked up some kindling. He threw on the embers to revive the fire and deposited two larger pieces of wood so that his embers would last until the morning.

He took his staff and went to the waterfall. He drank some water and then urinated below the reservoir, in the current. The water would take the odor of your urine away, avoiding attracting animals and possible visits from unexpected people. As quickly as he left, he returned to the crack. He lifted the door and tied it. He leaned on his arm and was quick to fall asleep, still thinking about the strange dream he had just had. Through the treetops the clouds ran quickly in front of the Moon and announced the wind to come. A few minutes after falling asleep, another cry similar to the one that had woken him cut across the valley. Echoing and silencing after a few moments. This time he did not wake up, as he slept soundly. He was very tired and apparently none of that would wake him up for the rest of the night.

Just before dawn he woke up. The day was just beginning to clear and I was already on my feet. He was hungry, but decided to go to the trap only after taking a little longer walk to see what was in the area. He took his staff and went up the slope. The trees at the top of the slope were more widely spaced apart, so I could see farther away than at the bottom. But even though the spacing between the trees was greater, he ended up concluding that, if he wanted to see in the distance, he would have to climb one of them to have a better view of the valley. He found an old tree of good altitude and climbed it to the top. It took a long time to get that done, but when he finished and looked around he was surprised and almost fell.

The forest in which it was found only existed on a narrow strip of land along the coast. Entering the continent a few dozen kilometers, the vegetation changed to a type of savanna or desert. I wasn't sure. Further on, after the desert, you can see a huge chain of white peaks covered by snow. The view from that point was privileged. On one side I could see the vastness of the ocean and in a single turn the beauty and grandeur of the mountains. He was afraid, because the extent of those lands was much greater than he had imagined. He had to better assess his next steps or he could end up dead in that desert. He stayed there for a while longer, without thinking too much about things. He just looked at the view and it calmed him down.

He decided to go down and headed for the trap. Hopefully I would have a good breakfast. And he was in luck, because when he got there he found a small wild bird trapped. It looked like a pigeon, but a little bigger. He didn't think twice: He took the animal and killed it instantly. He rearranged the trap and headed towards the crack to prepare his long-awaited food. There were apparently only ashes left in the fire. He threw some of the grass on which he had slept and, cleaning the ashes, placed them in the center of the circle of stones. In a short time a smoke formed and at that moment he put more wood on the grass and left. He knew that when he returned, the fire would be lit.

He also knew that if the bird's feathers burned, the strong and characteristic smell could attract animals or people, and this was not the time for any kind of encounter. He went to the waterfall and mixing water with a little earth made a little clay. He wrapped the pigeon with the clay without any of its feathers being exposed. He went back to the fire, which was already alive again. He opened a smaller hole in the middle of it and placed the coated bird in the middle, bringing the wood closer together and adding more wood.

For the next hour and a half, he should just sit and wait for the animal to be roasted. It was after nine o'clock in the morning when he leaned against one of the rocks that formed his shelter. He felt a soft but constant pain in his back. Had he been injured in the shipwreck that had brought him here? He tried to force his mind and remember the details of what he had been through before he got to where he was. He could only remember flashes of some older facts, from his childhood. When he tried to remember specific facts, his head hurt. He decided to wait for his memories to come back naturally.

He felt a little tired. His eyes were slowly closing until he dozed. It seemed to yield to that moment of relaxation. His body was still recovering and needed moments like that to complete total rehabilitation. But his peace did not last long. He woke up suddenly, seeming to hear something moving on dry leaves not far from his position. He paid more attention. They came from behind, to the right. The sound was getting closer every moment. He held his staff firmly, for at any moment he would be face to face with whatever was coming his way.

He tried to empty his mind. He was aware that emotional involvement during a fight was a disadvantage. He leaned further on the rock and, keeping his eyes fixed on the right, slowly pulled his legs out. The sound was very close. He prepared himself so that there would be no fight, that is, he planned to end everything with a single, sure stroke of his staff.

He was amazed when a little girl passed him without seeing him there. It was just a little girl dressed in multicolored outfits. Her skin was red and her hair was very black and straight, braided back. Her astonishment left him petrified, asking in thoughts that she should not see him. But his prayers were not answered. The girl turned around, as if looking for something, and immediately saw him leaning against the rock. She was so astonished when he was, and for a moment, also petrified. But his silence was short-lived, for he gave a shrill cry to which the answer was the murmur of countless voices coming his way.

With a sudden stop of the bus, he woke up almost with his face pressed to the floor.

- How many strange dreams will I still have? He thought to himself.

The only fact that comforted him was that they were already in the village. Incredibly achieved the feat of sleeping for the entire trip. Upon disembarking he received a dozen looks that were not welcome. Some people were not content with just disapproving looks, but also gave harsh words. Still others, as incredible as it might seem, plucked their eyelashes and tossed them. He felt very uncomfortable by that situation. He tried to speed up the pace, as he wanted to get to the cabin as soon as possible.

He was glad to have bought the bottle of whiskey. Without a drink it would be difficult to endure the whole situation. I would like to be able to relax a little in your friend's hut without having those worries. Perhaps now that he owned the weapon he could stay there without fear of being attacked again. As he walked through the village, his gaze was looking for Estela. But I felt that she was not around. I was unsure whether to go directly to the cabin or pass the infirmary. But it was not difficult for him to decide to go to the infirmary again to thank him for his help. If he got up the courage, he could ask her out for a drink in his cabin. But women usually don't like whiskey, I should have brought a wine maybe.

On the way he traveled, the people he came across had the most diverse reactions. Some looked at him with fear, others said words that he did not understand or proceeded with that bizarre vision of plucking his eyelashes. Luckily he was already at the door to the infirmary. He was happy because he saw the lights on and heard noise inside. The wind coming down from the mountains was still very cold. It funneled as it entered the city streets, forming a veritable icy corridor.

Once again he felt like returning to the house. Certainly in Brazil the temperature would be much more pleasant. He remained for a moment wondering what she would say about the weapon. He thought of going to the cabin and returning there another time. But he didn't resist: he knocked on the door. He knew that by the time it was already, he would not be able to go to the cabin before nightfall. And sleeping there in the open was not part of his plans. Hopefully she could offer you shelter for another night.

Estela opened the door. He looked extremely tired. The deep look and tousled hair were infallible evidence of his condition. It took a while to connect his image to the person, but when he came to his senses and saw that it was Victor, he opened his eyes wide with astonishment, saying a little clipped:

- You really came back ?!

- Yes. He replied skeptically for being disappointed by the reception. Some problem?

- Only one. The whole city thinks you are to blame for the problems of some residents.

- What? He said in amazement. What are they based on to affirm this? Finally he stammered. And you, what do you think?

- I do not know what to say. But deep down she knew and continued. You may not be prepared to accept other people's truth.

- I'm sorry, but I'll tell you what I'm thinking at the moment. She looked him in the eye and waited for him to complete his sentence. I'm cold and hungry, so I'm willing to willingly accept a plate of your soup. She said pointing to the table behind her. During dinner we can thoroughly discuss our differences in point of view. What do you think?

He disliked his approach, but noticing his tiredness from the trip and a background of sincerity in his words, Estela gestured for him to get out of the cold and enter.

- As you will notice for yourself, we only have a little soup to share. I was getting ready for dinner right now and alone.

- No problem! In town I bought some packages of instant food and we can increase the quantity of your soup by adding one of these envelopes.

From the face she made, as if she hated that kind of food. He noticed that it was not a good solution to the problem.

- But if you don't like this type of food, I also brought some bread. They must be a little dented, but they are from today. What do you think?

- And you still ask? Bring the bread.

Estela took the pot and brought it back to the fire to heat it up. All that time talking together with the cold it made the soup cool.

- Sit there on the sofa while the soup is heating up. She said seeing him standing beside her like a statue.

- It's ok. He said confirming with an indication in the direction of the sofa.

He was feeling better at that moment. The warmth of the house, not only that of the fireplace, but the human warmth with which she had received him in spite of everything were doing her good. It had been awhile since she had felt right in one place. While waiting for his thoughts they drove him home. He thought he had left his home to be able to forget the stressful moments of work and ended up being very stressed there. A funny situation, given the contradiction. He moved his head over his shoulders, relaxing even more. He closed his eyes for a moment.

Estela came by to ask him to eat. He thought he was dozing and wanted to leave him there, without disturbing his sleep. But when he turned around he heard the sound of his feet and opened his eyes.

- The smell is not the best, hopefully the taste compensates. He said in a playful tone.

- Define "not the best" and be careful what you say or you will only eat mashed bread.

Seeing that she was serious, he tried to find a good argument for his off-time joke.

- For this type of food, when prepared, the most diverse flavors result in almost the same aroma. We can't tell if it's good or bad. I can only tell you that, according to expectations, she is strange.

She seemed to think for a moment, trying to understand everything he had said to her, but her tiredness outweighed her patience.

- Since I don't have the time or the will to understand everything you said to me. I have nothing more to say, the taste of my dish will do this for me. Let's eat?

- Clear!

Victor cut the bread into slices and placed it on a separate plate. After the soup was served, they began to eat in silence. For about ten minutes in the house, the wind could only be heard trying to get in through the cracks and hissing in anger at not being able to. The silence had not been noticed by the two, as they were concerned with the events that had passed and were yet to come. Victor broke the silence with one of his many inopportune phrases.

- Good thing that there are still things that manage to surprise me.

- I'll take this as a compliment.

- And it was. He said smiling.

- I need to talk to you about a very serious matter! When he finished saying these words, his countenance changed.

- You can talk. He said, still smiling, not allowing himself to be taken seriously by her.

- I'm very worried! Partly because I don't know if I'll get you to understand me. On the other hand, you were totally skeptical when we talked about this earlier. I want you to know that I care about you.

- There you go again with your fantastic ideas. I said interrupting her.

- These are not fantastic ideas. What I am trying to explain to you has been part of the local culture for over two thousand years. If something has survived that long you have to agree that some real fund has it.

- If we used this argument of yours on other matters, you yourself would see that you said a great nonsense. It came out so fast that when he realized what he had said it was too late.

- Okay, Victor, I won't waste our time anymore! You haven't even heard what I have to say to you and have already built your walls. I'm going to sleep right here today and if you want to stay you can use the sofa.

Saying this, she frowned. Victor realized that she had been angry and because of the little he knew about women, he thought he would not talk to him for at least the next two hours. I knew it wouldn't matter if I tried to explain myself, or if I apologized for what I said. Not even if he said he would hear what she had to say. She wouldn't be back to normal until that time passed. It might even make your situation worse. As it was late, I was sure I would not speak to her again until the next day.

She went to her room and picked up a thick cotton blanket, with brightly colored lines and a predominance of red. He handed it to Victor and pointed to the sofa. After the events, and since it was already late, it was dangerous to walk the trail that led to the cabin at that time. Very conveniently, he had no trouble accepting the offer. Partly because of the tiredness I felt, but also because of the need to have someone else's company.

Estela realized that he would be fine if he went to his room, closed the door and a few seconds later he can hear the clear sound of the lock being turned, as if to say:

- Don't bother me, because I'm very angry!

He laughed to himself and turned to the sofa. He was very happy to have his company and to be able to trust her. This was enough to sleep thankfully. Already lying down he began to reflect and realized that after the attack he had suffered he had not slept in a normal place. They were just sofas, bus seats, infirmary beds. He shook his head, for he knew that despite everything he should be grateful. He might be dead, but instead he was fine and he had met a very special person. A true friend.

He thought again of Brazil, of his home, of his loved ones. Everything seemed to be another reality, another life. Everything that he had lived up to the moment did not seem to be part of his current life. Except for him and his way of being, he saw no connection between the two stories. If they were films, they would be meaningless compared. It didn't take long for the light on the lamp to go out and from that moment on he couldn't help falling asleep.

As soon as he had found a pleasant position on the sofa and started to lull himself in his sleep, he heard a knock on the door. He sat on the sofa and was silent to pay better attention. For a few minutes he remained inert, barely breathing, but he heard nothing. He lay down again.

- It must have been the wind! He thought.

He turned and when he dozed he heard a new knock, this time harder. He looked at his watch, it was after two in the morning. He found it strange, as he had the perception that he had just gone to bed. It was also strange that someone was hitting that hour. But he remembered that he was in a doctor's office. The only one in the entire region. He found it natural to knock on his door loudly at night to ask for help. Estela should be used to it by now, for sure she would soon be there to answer the door. He lay down and turned to try to sleep again.

A much louder crash than the previous beats can be heard. His breathing was faster.

- Adrenaline! Thought.

He stopped breathing for a moment in order to listen more carefully to what was happening. Nothing! No one calling or asking for help. A new knock shook the floor of the house. The sound made him jump off the couch and get to his feet. From the noise that followed it, it looked like something had broken. It certainly came from Estela's bedroom window. He ran to get his gun, but his backpack was not where he left it. Estela could have picked her up so he wouldn't leave without talking to her in the morning.

- Focus, Victor! Focus! He told himself.

I knew I should remain calm. In times of despair our brain acts impulsively. He shouted at Estela's bedroom door to open it. She answered nothing. He turned the handle, but none of the door opened. He remembered that she had locked the door from the inside. The sound of things being broken inside the room meant that he had to make a quick decision.

He started kicking the door with all the strength he had, but it was very old and massive wood, instead of knocking the door down he was managing to hurt his foot. He took his distance and, running, gave a shoulder to the door that did not resist and burst into the lock that was rusty. He was taken aback by the opening of the door and rolled on the floor of the dark room. I couldn't see anything in there.

When he got up he realized he was wet. He took the lantern he had dropped and rekindled it, he realized it was not water. It was reddish. It was. Blood!

He was all bloody! The floor was covered in blood! The sight was terrifying, his feet could barely move. The whole room was destroyed, only the bed remained in place. Intact! Untouched!

He heard the sound of something moving under the bed. He overcame his fear and slowly approached to see what it was. I was very scared, but I had to see what was there. It could be Estela, hurt and in need of help. He lifted the sheet and to his horror there was nothing there. He knelt down to get a closer look.

The vision he would witness was too much: Estela's head lay there. Only the head! Eyes and ears plucked out. As if it had been left on purpose. In the little part of the neck that was left, the form of tearing could be seen: It had been torn off!

It seemed that an extreme force had held and pulled her, until it detached from the rest of the body. Victor started to come to himself and felt nauseous, only now becoming aware. He felt that he could not bear all that pressure, and he let out a cry of despair so loud that the whole village could hear it and he was terrified.

FIVE

As was already common in those days, she woke up with a start, all sweaty and staring at him was Estela.

- Stay calm. She said, looking not nervous. It was just another dream. Nothing happened to me, I'm fine!

He embraced her involuntarily and took a breath, seeming to regain his sanity.

"But how do you know my dream was about you?"

Looking closely at her, he noticed that her right arm was bandaged. Blood from the wounds was beginning to seep through the bandage gauze. He pointed to the wound, but before he asked she said:

- The night before, while you were unconscious, something came out the window. She was very nervous when speaking and her voice came out with difficulty. I was in my room, more excited to have talked and see that it got better. I noticed a sudden gust of wind at the window and went to it to finish closing it. Suddenly it exploded over me and I was knocked over. I don't remember anything after that. I woke up at the home of one of the residents, with this wound on my arm. They told me that they heard a scream and that when they arrived I was lying on the floor of the room unconscious with these wounds on my arm. They said it was the same animal that attacked you. They saw nothing but me, but they said that the fact that I took care of you caused the creature to come to punish me too.

Victor stood for a moment without saying anything, only reflecting on the things she had said and the events he had been going through during those days. He considered himself a very knowledgeable man, on a number of subjects, but all the problems he had faced and the experiences he had acquired up to that moment were of no help to him.

Everything that came from her previous life, as she now considered it, was worthless there. This was something new, coming from this new life and it was not logical. He was fleeing his limited field of vision. It was out of his domain. He felt very bad, very distressed, because he had never before found himself in a situation where he was so needy. He wanted to cry. He felt dizzy and stopped for a moment to ask God, with whom he had not spoken in years, that if that were a dream, that He would have mercy and wake him up. The world he believed in, in which he had grown up, was disappearing. Giving way to something unknown and that scared him. He rubbed his eyes and shook his head with quick movements to try to compose himself.

- Which one. What is your opinion about what they are saying? He asked as if in a last attempt to understand everything he was going through. He began to accept that he might have to forget everything he believed.

- Since I arrived here, around seven years ago, I have seen and witnessed a series of events that make me take the things that the natives say very seriously.

- But what do they say is happening?

- Well, they say that this creature or animal, as you want to call it, is chasing you because you were cursed.

- But. How cursed? He hesitated. Because?

- They say you have something like a debt to the gods. I don't know what kind of debt, I don't know what gods. Please don't ask me any more! They just told me this. I didn't understand it either.

- I will not believe such nonsense! He retaliated. Cursed for what? By whom? When? This does not make sense.

- They say the only solution is for you to leave the lands of the Empire of the Four Worlds.

- Empire of what? What are you talking about?

- I don't know the story well, but before the Spaniards arrived in Latin America; the Incas who lived in the current region of Peru, Ecuador, Bolivia, Argentina and Chile, mainly, formed an empire so vast that they found it convenient to divide it into four parts: The Four Corners of the World or the Four Worlds only. Tahuantinsuyo in Quechua, the local language.

- Should I leave these lands, and will my problems end? It's just this?

- According to them.

- Nor are you convinced of this! You can tell in the way you speak.

- That's not it! I'm like this because I don't want you to leave! He said at last.

That was a surprise to him. He had suddenly realized why she was concerned. He was silent, looking straight into her eyes. After a few seconds he lowered his head and rested it on his hands in exhaustion. I didn't know what to say or what to do. He felt his hands were tied.

- I don't know if it will work, but. She continued in a calmer tone. They told me that maybe there is another way to solve the problem.

It took a while for his words to be heard by him, who was deep in thought. But he saw that he had gotten his attention by raising his head.

- Like? What other way?

- The natives told me that there is an old Inca priest, whom they call "Uillac Uma". They say he is a type of healer who, according to them, has special powers and the ancient knowledge needed to help us.

- How do you help us? I thought the problem was just mine.

- I think I'm also part of the problem. I am your friend and I will not leave you alone in this.

Victor fell silent again. I had to make a decision and I knew it. I also had to reflect on it, as it would influence other people's lives. He had always been faithful to his intuitions, but at that moment he knew that they would not help him. He looked at Estela, who was patiently awaiting the end of her reflection. He looked at her and felt something he had never felt before: That he could entrust his life to her!

- Do you trust the judgment of these people? Asked Estela.

- Yes! He answered immediately. Since I came here, I have seen very strange things, which the people here have managed, in their own way, to resolve. Yes, I believe their word!

- I would like you to know that I trust you! Something tells me that I shouldn't just turn my back on this and run. So, if you tell me that I must do what you say, I agree. Although I don't understand what's going on, I still think we could solve all of this with a little more logic or.

- Okay, Victor. She spoke quickly to take advantage of the opportunity he had given her. Glad to see you agreed. I want you to get some rest. He said suddenly looking like he was in a hurry. I am going out to consult some people who can help.

Victor looked at her like he was about to give up on everything and walk out the door without any major concerns. But before he could say anything Estela led him to his room to see the shattered window, showing him that it was real and very serious. Before he could say anything, she turned and left.

He returned to the living room and sat on the sofa. He wondered if what he was about to do was correct. Could there be another, less radical and more logical solution? But he didn't have time to start listing the other likely solutions. Estela was already back and panted through the door for running. He had a piece of paper in his hands.

- We have to get ready and leave in half an hour at most. Otherwise, we may not arrive at our destination until nightfall. She said quickly, struggling to get her breath back.

- But now? Today? He asked, stunned.

- We have to resolve this as soon as possible! It is not the kind of thing left for tomorrow.

Seeing Estela's determined look at what to do and realizing that he couldn't change her mind, he nodded.

- Go packing your things I need to do something before we leave.

Again before he could say a word, she was gone. Then he did what he could: packed his bag. He prepared the weapon and everything was ready. We just need something to eat now, he thought. He was going to look around to see if he found anything, but he decided to wait for Estela. Maybe she would be angry if she found him snooping around in her kitchen cabinets.

About ten minutes passed and he was again enveloped in thoughts that went round and round. They came and went and took him nowhere. Nothing clear about how I should proceed.

- How is it? Is ready? She said as she hurried through the door.

- Yes. We just need something to eat.

- Here it is.

She handed him two packages that appeared to contain homemade bread. He quickly gathered two blankets and a change of clothes. He put things in his backpack, leaving the blankets out. It was the opposite example of what Victor used to see in women, who usually took hours to get dressed. In less than five minutes of preparation, she was ready.

- Take these things and put them in your backpack. She said, not wanting to waste time.

- No problem. Victor replied a little disbelievingly.

They left the house and she locked the door. The streets they passed were empty. Looking ahead, Victor could see some people, but when they saw them approaching, they continued to enter their homes quickly.

- Our farewell committee! He said.

He had already gotten used to the treatment. Estela arranged with one of the inhabitants, who had a tractor, to take them to a stretch from which the tractor was unable to travel. From there they would continue on foot to that healer's hut. They both sat at the back of a trailer that the man apparently used to transport grass, manure or move plants.

The dirt in which he found himself was indescribable. Victor thought that if the animal that chased them had the least sense of cleanliness, it certainly wouldn't come after them. And he laughed to himself. Aside from the bumps that the trailer gave when it passed through the potholes, the journey continued calmly. The landscape was very beautiful. The mountains in the background with their snow covered peaks. He had been there for a long time, but he was still enchanted by that look. I could not count the number of peaks, as they overlapped and one after another disappeared on the horizon, forming something similar to a fog.

He wondered what could be hidden in these mountains. He had read that in the days of greater heat and better visibility, people on commercial flights over the mountain range, viewed buildings inside the craters of the sleeping volcanoes. There were peoples, prior to the Incas, who worshiped volcanoes as deities. Attributing myths about the creation of the world to them. These peoples built their places of worship next to their supposed gods, inside.

It would be a very interesting discovery to find these supposed places, he thought. Many scholars said that the difficulty was in the countless number of places of this type that the mountain range kept. In addition to many of these volcanoes having a very thick layer of ice, others had their peaks destroyed by earthquakes.

Added to the difficulty that "normal" human beings have to survive in these places. Normal, since the natives of the high altitudes of the Andes have adaptations to the conditions that allow them to perform better than people from other places. As an example of this, we have the blood of these people who have adapted, allowing them to breathe more easily in thin air and with less oxygen from these places.

Other problems are: low plant nutrition, constant cold in all seasons and aridity. It is a semi-desert climate, with very little rainfall and the existence of water only through melting ice. He imagined what it would be like for an entire people to adapt to life in this type of place. The reasons that led them to establish housing in these places should really be very serious. In order to accept that as a reality to live with on a daily basis, a series of paradigms should be broken. Estela remained silent, looking concerned. Always looking at your watch.

- What will happen when we get to this person's house? Asked Victor, making conversation.

- We will tell him the whole story and he will guide us on what we should do to solve the problem. She said dryly without stretching.

- Only that? No major complications?

- Yes, it's that simple.

- And what do you think he will tell us to do? He insisted without paying any attention to her condition.

- I can not even imagine. In fact, I don't even know if we can find this man.

- What you mean? Never been to the place before?

- Neither me nor anyone in the village!

- And how do you know he's where they say? How are you sure of its existence?

- I don't know if it's there, and I'm not sure it really exists! I just know that this is our only chance. And we have to try.

- Very cool! He blew up. We are in the body of a tractor in pieces, looking for a person that we do not know if it exists, solving a problem that we do not know if we have. That was all that was missing to complete.

"Very well!"

- At last he got real. She thought, remaining silent, knowing that her reaction would be something like this.

As he was ignored, he turned to look at the landscape, since all that was left of him was comfort. On second thought, he imagined that nothing would happen to them and in the worst of circumstances he would take a hike in the mountains in the company of a beautiful woman. That was also a great reason to be around. He stopped thinking about the problems. He made a mental effort to get rid of them. He decided to try to seize the moment. Live life, as adventurers say. He was aware that he could, as anyone can, condition himself to the mood he desired. Your brain was the basis for any kind of feeling you wanted. If you let yourself be carried away by the moment and became sad and sorry, you just let yourself go and be conditioned to that. On the other hand, if you were to think positively and strive to feel better, you would certainly be able to see your positives in the situation.

The wind was getting hotter and hotter, he started to feel hot and decided to take off his shirt. They had been on the tractor for over three hours. He watched the man taking them. He had the typical appearance of people in the village. He was reddish-skinned, with thick, straight black hair, cut in a straight line just below his ears. It was covered with a colorful poncho, tied by a rope braided at the waist. His features were undoubtedly purely indigenous. And this was not very common in Argentina, as in other countries in Spanish South America.

A short time later the man turned and said a few words to Estela. Victor couldn't hear. Apparently he showed her something in the distance. Estela in turn was better positioned on the transport to check what it was about. Victor wasn't too worried, he knew she would tell him if something serious was going on. A few minutes after they ended their conversation, Estela took out her backpack.

- Are we going down? Victor asked.

- Yes, two more kilometers and the tractor will have to return!

Victor noticed that they had climbed a lot and from where they were, it was easier to see the mountain peaks. He was having trouble breathing and the peaks that had previously looked like a fog were now beginning to take shape.

- Here! Chew or you'll start to feel really bad.

- What is this?

- Coca leaves! At these altitudes that we will be going through we will need them very much.

- If my doctor is referring you.

He put the leaf in his mouth and started chewing, as if it were a regular gum. He could feel the grandeur of the place. The tractor had followed for a good part of the time on a dirt road and then through the middle of a field where the vegetation was some kind of grass. Looking down in the distance, he saw points that resembled the village from which they left. Thinking a little, he found it unlikely to be. They had followed very winding places and it was certainly not possible to see it from that point. It must have been some kind of escarpment or bush of a different color. He wasn't sure, nor did he care much about it.

The tractor stopped without warning, causing the two to be thrown against the woods on the side of the cart. For a brief moment he can feel the warmth of Estela's body. The sensation was the most comforting he had experienced since the moment that all those strange things started to happen to him. She looked him deeply in the eye before being caught in a reflex, which threw her back and separated from him.

He jumped off the tractor and the driver did not wait for Victor to descend. He turned and, had he not actually jumped on the move, he would have started descending again at full speed back to the starting point. The driver screamed, saying goodbye and was returned by Estela. Victor thought it was all very strange, but he didn't even dare to ask. He stopped watching the tractor descent, and did not even notice that Estela was already striding about ten meters in front of him. When he looked for Estela he saw her walking in the distance and had to run a long way to reach her.

She really was in a hurry. He thought. He called to her, who indicated with a hand gesture that he should come faster, as he would not slow down to wait for her. He accelerated his pace and ran for a while, until he got closer to her.

- Why do we have to run? He asked, still breathless.

- We're not running. We're moving fast.

- Why do we have to walk fast?

- Because it's almost ten o'clock and we haven't even met halfway.

The footsteps were tiring him more and more and he felt his bruised muscles aching. At all times he looked at his watch to see if the hour passed, but it did not. It was the opposite for her: with each new look towards the sun, it seemed to her that several hours had passed.

They walked for about two hours and Victor started to wonder if it would be time to stop for a while to eat and rest. In the end, I wasn't sure if that crazy race would make any sense. I was in the mood to stop, but I knew that if I asked Estela about that possibility, she would certainly go crazy! He decided to eat a small snack, walking. Lifting his head and looking a little higher, he noticed the peculiar landscape of the trail and decided to focus on it to try not to worry about the weather anymore.

The weather was still too cold for his standards and looking at the lighter parts of the landscape he could feel his eyes sting. The snow-capped mountain peaks looked like they had been hand painted by the creator. And there were also the small streams that flowed from above with its transparent, icy and refreshing waters. He slowed down next to one of these streams, washed his hands in the water and passed over his face and neck. That was very invigorating. That water was very energetic, because it gave her an extra boost to reach Estela who did not slow down the accelerated stride.

Looking around he noticed several species of plants that he had never seen before. They were very different from those I knew in Brazil. The climate in which he usually lived was practically tropical, and now he was in a tropical region too, but with high altitude. Which greatly changed the characteristic of plants for their survival: With thinner foliage so as not to lose heat and humidity, and with lighter shades than dark greens due to the luminosity.

The altitude also greatly changed the characteristics of the plants, which were mostly flat. With some trees spaced that could be considered shrubs. He plucked a leaf through which he passed and saw that it was thick, and filled with a gel that when squeezed turned into a liquid. He imagined that these were energy reserves for times of scarcity of humidity and sunlight.

His stomach started to remind him that he hadn't eaten anything very significant until that moment. He wondered when they were going to stop to rest and eat for real. But I was still afraid to approach Estela. Deep down, what he didn't want was to show weaknesses around her. Even so, and as he was curious to know about Estela, he decided to start a conversation in another way. And if the subject allowed it, it would address tiredness and hunger.

- Why did you decide to come here to practice medicine? At this point, he would realize the degree of annoyance he was in. She waited for a sharp answer, but instead she spoke normally.

- Well. At the time I started my medical residency there was an exchange program at the college that needed volunteers for the job. It was a period that should have lasted a year and then I would go back to Brazil. When I started I received a post in a town about fifty miles from the village, and I confess that I didn't like it very much. In the third month I couldn't take it anymore and I wanted to leave everything and go home.

She paused, as if focusing on a part of the trail where there seemed to be two paths to follow. He quickly decided on the part that rose between two rocks and continued on long strides.

- My supervisor at the hospital was very attentive and realized that I was unmotivated. One day he called me, saying that I was very independent in the decisions I made and the cases I took care of. And trying to captivate me, he praised my work and the way I treated people. It was the day before my break. He asked me if I would like to take care of an outpost, alone. He said he didn't need to answer at that moment and gave me the address of the place. He also gave me the post's key and said that it had been deactivated for almost a year, because no one had adapted there. He said that the natives of the region preserved the traces of their culture, that it was still very old and that in some cases they did not accept well the interventions of modern medicine. At the end of the conversation he even offered me a driver, in case I wanted to go there to see the place.

He had got it right! His mood was much better. She even seemed a little excited. At this point, she pointed to the right at the top, and at about eight hundred meters he could see a huge waterfall. It consisted of three falls in a row. The strong wind and the undulations of the terrain covered her sound and for this reason he was very surprised to see that image suddenly.

- Very beautiful. Shall we move closer to her? Asked Victor.

- No. From this point we started to go further north.

- What a pity. But continue your story. It was interesting!

- On my break I had nothing to do, as it was the only program in the city and I decided to go to that outpost. I didn't ask the driver or I would have to go and come back quickly, and that wasn't what I was thinking. If he decided to stay, he needed to know the city before making the decision. I prepared a small backpack with clothes for two days and left. I took a bus just before lunch and two hours later disembarked at the site. My initial impression was also not very good. But I tried to keep thinking positive. I asked the people at the bus stop about the address indicated and they pointed me to an alley about two hundred meters away. My impression was that I was in an indigenous village, but as I had a Brazilian concept of village: thatched houses arranged in a circle, with half-naked people with children on their lap and smoking their pipes. And without realizing it, he smiled. I soon dismissed the idea and thought in terms of a small town. Before, I had broken my paradigms and kept the idea of a tribe.

- I don't know if I understood correctly, but you want to tell me that that village is, in fact, an indigenous village? He asked in surprise, looking like he was really interested.

- Yes, without a doubt! Estela said naturally. It is a common confusion among us who do not know the indigenous peoples of the regions of the Andes. They build with stone, and use foliage and branches to cover the houses. They arrange their houses in an aligned way, usually in relation to the cardinal points. They control the weather and seasons very precisely. The Sun is your main God. There in the village it is still called in the ancient language of the Incas, Quechua. She looked at Victor to see if she was being heard. And with the confirmation of his gaze, which showed much attention, he decided to continue.

- Arriving at the office I realized that it had been a long time since the last time the door had been opened. The locks were rusty and full of dust that made me sneeze. I was horrified to imagine that there was a possibility that the place was covered in mold. He was really reluctant and remained outside for a long time. I lost patience with myself and went inside. I started to hope that the lamps would work and after a few winks they took strength and filled the room with their light. I walked through every room and realized they were a little messy. His ordering was not the best for the service. At that moment an old man appeared at the door, who for a moment looked me straight in the eye, seeming to read my memories or thoughts. I was embarrassed and looked away asking if I could help.

"- I need you to come with me and take a look at a person. Said the old man, very calmly and serenely in his voice. "

"- I'm just doing a conference at the post. I don't know if I will come to work here. I said trying not to get involved with work yet. "

- He looked me in the eye again and said something that, every time I remember, I feel my body shiver.

"- We both know that your decision has already been made. This person really needs your help now and will not be able to wait for his return. "

She paused and her gaze was far away. Recovering the memories and perhaps still trying to understand what had happened. He immediately came to himself, continuing.

She paused, as if focusing on a part of the trail where there seemed to be two paths to follow. He quickly decided on the part that rose between two rocks and continued on long strides.

- My supervisor at the hospital was very attentive and realized that I was unmotivated. One day he called me, saying that I was very independent in the decisions I made and the cases I took care of. And trying to captivate me, he praised my work and the way I treated people. It was the day before my break. He asked me if I would like to take care of an outpost, alone. He said he didn't need to answer at that moment and gave me the address of the place. He also gave me the post's key and said that it had been deactivated for almost a year, because no one had adapted there. He said that the natives of the region preserved the traces of their culture, that it was still very old and that in some cases they did not accept well the interventions of modern medicine. At the end of the conversation he even offered me a driver, in case I wanted to go there to see the place.

He had got it right! His mood was much better. She even seemed a little excited. At this point, she pointed to the right at the top, and at about eight hundred meters he could see a huge waterfall. It consisted of three falls in a row. The strong wind and the undulations of the terrain covered her sound and for this reason he was very surprised to see that image suddenly.

- Very beautiful. Shall we move closer to her? Asked Victor.

- No. From this point we started to go further north.

- What a pity. But continue your story. It was interesting!

- On my break I had nothing to do, as it was the only program in the city and I decided to go to that outpost. I didn't ask the driver or I would have to go and come back quickly, and that wasn't what I was thinking. If he decided to stay, he needed to know the city before making the decision. I prepared a small backpack with clothes for two days and left. I took a bus just before lunch and two hours later disembarked at the site. My initial impression was also not very good. But I tried to keep thinking positive. I asked the people at the bus stop about the address indicated and they pointed me to an alley about two hundred meters away. My impression was that I was in an indigenous village, but as I had a Brazilian concept of village: thatched houses arranged in a circle, with half-naked people with children on their lap and smoking their pipes. And without realizing it, he smiled. I soon dismissed the idea and thought in terms of a small town. Before, I had broken my paradigms and kept the idea of a tribe.

- I don't know if I understood correctly, but you want to tell me that that village is, in fact, an indigenous village? He asked in surprise, looking like he was really interested.

- Yes, without a doubt! Estela said naturally. It is a common confusion among us who do not know the indigenous peoples of the regions of the Andes. They build with stone, and use foliage and branches to cover the houses. They arrange their houses in an aligned way, usually in relation to the cardinal points. They control the weather and seasons very precisely. The Sun is your main God. There in the village it is still called in the ancient language of the Incas, Quechua. She looked at Victor to see if she was being heard. And with the confirmation of his gaze, which showed much attention, he decided to continue.

- Arriving at the office I realized that it had been a long time since the last time the door had been opened. The locks were rusty and full of dust that made me sneeze. I was horrified to imagine that there was a possibility that the place was covered in mold. He was really reluctant and remained outside for a long time. I lost patience with myself and went inside. I started to hope that the lamps would work and after a few winks they took strength and filled the room with their light. I walked through every room and realized they were a little messy. His ordering was not the best for the service. At that moment an old man appeared at the door, who for a moment looked me straight in the eye, seeming to read my memories or thoughts. I was embarrassed and looked away asking if I could help.

"- I need you to come with me and take a look at a person. Said the old man, very calmly and serenely in his voice. "

"- I'm just doing a conference at the post. I don't know if I will come to work here. I said trying not to get involved with work yet. "

- He looked me in the eye again and said something that, every time I remember, I feel my body shiver.

"- We both know that your decision has already been made. This person really needs your help now and will not be able to wait for his return. "

She paused and her gaze was far away. Recovering the memories and perhaps still trying to understand what had happened. He immediately came to himself, continuing.

- I wasn't sure what to do, so I accompanied him to a small house near the central part of the village. When I got there I noticed that there were eight people in a room. Everyone looked at me in amazement. I don't think they saw anyone outside the village in a while. Some moved away, but a very old lady stood between me and what appeared to be a large curtain of fabric. And when the old man asked her to leave he made a negative sign. At this moment, they started a tense conversation where I was totally embarrassed, because I didn't understand what they were talking about. They started talking in Quechua! But at that time I didn't know and I was very surprised. A few minutes later the man seemed to use the hierarchy and the woman left with her head down as she passed him. But he looked up and looked at me when he passed me.

"- Everything fine now! Said the old man motioning for me to follow him. "

- We passed through the fabric partition and in the dark room we entered I could see a small bed where a young woman of about fourteen lay. She was very thin and had deep dark circles. When I approached she was startled and started to babble words she couldn't understand. She was burning with fever. I also noticed a large blood stain on the bed, about waist level, just below. It was almost completely dry, but it left a very strong smell in the room. And talking about it, I seem to return to that moment.

"- We have to take her to the office. I saw a room there that will be much better to maintain and faster to do some tests. "

- I realized then that the old man was not happy with the idea of having to remove the girl from there.

"- You asked me to help, didn't you? And he nodded. "

"- So I need you to help me too. She is very weak and I am not sure that we will be able to save her. But I am sure that in this room we will have less chance than if we take her to the infirmary. "

The man seemed to think for a moment. At the end, he nodded and said:

"- We will do it your way, but I will be with her all the time!"

"- Okay, because I will need someone to help me."

- We decided to use the bed on which she rested to transport it. We decided to pin his body to the bed so he wouldn't fall. And when everything was ready the old man went out and called other residents to help load the bed, telling me at the end:

"- Go ahead! We will arrive soon. It is better not to be seen with us at this point. "

- I agreed with a nod and went quickly to the office. The problem was, he didn't know what she had, nor did he have a clue how to treat it. I confess that for a moment I wished I never went to that place. I had never lost anyone and I didn't want it to be there. But before the feeling of fear could come over me, the old man and two men appeared with the young woman. I asked them to put her in the bed she had in her room at the entrance to the office. At that moment the old man dismissed the men and approached me. I was preparing an injection to help cut the girl's fever.

"- Let's agree on something else. Said the old man. Do you do what you can for the health of the young woman's body that I will take care of the health of her spirit, combined? "

- I didn't quite understand what he wanted to say to me with that, but he said yes. He sat in a chair near the foot of the bed, closed his eyes and began to speak very quietly, apparently in the dialect I commented on. For a moment I was paralyzed, looking at him. Who stopped and looked at me too. I shook my head, apologizing, and continued with my work. I applied the medicine to cut the fever and hoped it would work. Not all medications react as we expect when we don't know the real reason for the fever. Fifteen minutes later she started to sweat a lot and her temperature increased, a reaction that was sometimes normal and sometimes bad. At this moment the old man started to speak a little louder and his eyes opened, but.

She paused for a moment, as if in doubt to proceed.

- Continue Estela. Said Victor. I `m listening you. Continue, please.

- They were white, they seemed to have lost their color. I looked intently for a moment but, as I had to pay attention to the young woman, I was unable to notice for a long time. Moments later, the sweat subsided and she settled down better on the bed. With the fever under control, I took his blood for some tests and found that he would need a transfusion. Luckily the office had an emergency transfusion kit. I took the tests and found that one of the men who had brought the girl before could be a donor without major consequences for both of them.

- We started the transfusion with a little fear on the part of the old man and the man. But we were lucky and everything went very well. On the blood test, I noticed that it could be a liver infection. And with the evident loss of blood in the bed, her picture could have worsened. I waited an hour after the end of the transfusion to avoid the risk of adverse reactions. Everything seemed to be normal, so I administered an antibiotic to the serum she was taking. At the next eight hours, it was the most difficult time I spent with the young woman. The old man stayed there the whole time.

- Always mumbling something that I couldn't understand. Now higher, now lower, now only as a slight whisper. I ended up falling asleep beside the girl's bed, in an old chair that was in the office. Sometime in the evening I ended up leaning my head back on the bed. At this moment I think I started to dream. I walked in a field with snow that started to melt. The grass appeared green and many flowers were beginning to bloom. When the image started to become clearer, I noticed two figures sitting on a stone, just above where I was.

- I walked towards the figures and I could see that they were a woman and a man. They were talking and laughing out loud. As I approached they were silent, waving my hand for me to approach. I went to meet them and was surprised when I saw that it was the young woman and the old man. I felt happy to be with them and started to talk. I stayed there for a long time. But at some point they both disappeared, and I was worried. I felt a light breeze in my hair and the reality seemed to pull me. When I realized I was in the office next to the young woman, who was stroking my hair.

"- Thanks! She said in a very weak voice. My name is Ianami. "

"- You're welcome."

- I was confused so I got up and went to the office reception. My back was crushed from sleeping in that position. There I met the old man, who looked much less worried than the day before.

"- We had an agreement yesterday, don't you remember? He asked."

"- Yes, of course I remember. She replied a little worried. "

"- Anyway, thank you very much for helping me."

"- It was nothing, all I did was take care of the health of the body, as we agreed."

"- It was not what I saw."

"- As well?"

"- Last night. When we were out in the field talking. "

"- As I said?"

- Aren't you going to tell me you forgot? It would be very sad. It would be a waste of your natural gift, Dr. I will rest for a while, but I'll be right back. Now, more than ever, I'm sure she is in good hands.

- Saying this he left and left me looking after the girl. After that day I was never able to leave those people again. I became friends with Ianami and helper. The whole village now looks like a big family to me.

He was very impressed by the story and was still trying to become aware of some excerpts when it completed:

- Shall we take a short break to rest and eat? What do you think of the idea?

Without thinking of anything else, Victor's own body responded, falling down immediately.

- I will understand this as a "yes". She said smiling.

SIX

The two leaned on a rock that was mostly covered with moss. As they were going up, they could now see far away and the feeling he had was that they were nothing more than grains of sand in the immensity of those mountains. Snowy peaks and peaks and countless repetitions as far as the eye can see. Some were so tall that they even touched the clouds.

- Very curious story that you just told me.

Estela was chewing something and made a sign that she needed some time to respond. He took the opportunity to look around again. He hadn't realized that right behind them there was a very tall tree that looked more than five hundred years old. It was, without a doubt, the largest and oldest among which they had passed so far. He started to think about something, but he heard Estela talking.

- It was the purest truth.

- I have no doubt that it is true. I just thought it was fantastic. There are many coincidences and that part related to the dream. it was very strange.

She looked him in the eye and realized that she would still encounter a lot of resistance until he believed all the things he needed. But I wasn't worried about it now. What worried her was whether they would be able to reach their destination in time. Victor, on the contrary, thought that she was already in a much better mood, so she wouldn't insist on logic at this point. The worst part, in her view, was that they had already been on the road for a while and she didn't even show a hint of tiredness. Estela continued to eat her meal.

- I was born and raised in the city of São Paulo, but my parents were from the interior of the state. They had moved to the capital for better job opportunities. But on vacation we would go to my grandparents' house for a few days. There everything seemed to be more cheerful and time seemed to stop. There was a lot of green and a small lake near my maternal grandparents' house. There we fished and fed the ducks. And there were also the stories they told. Where nature was always in evidence. She sighed and continued, seeing that she had Victor's attention.

- In short, when I helped save that young woman, I became known to everyone in the village and was welcomed as if I were in a large family. Unconditionally! This made me decide to take over the office and move there. And with a leap, seeming to return to reality, she added: Now that you know the story, we can continue on our journey!

- Wow, but already?

- Yes. We have to go or we won't be there in time. Do you see this mark here on the map?

- Yes. What is it about?

- More or less marks the middle of the road. Do you see this drawing close to the brand?

- Yes. It looks like a bush!

At this point she raised her right hand and pointed behind Victor. And if he turns around, he can contemplate the big tree he had seen before.

- You mean we're still halfway there? He said discouraged.

- That's why we need to speed up the pace. We will!

Saying this she got up and started walking without looking back. He had to collect his things in a hurry and run after her, who was already ten meters ahead of him. In the distance he could see the trail turning into a big curve, surrounding the mountain they were on. He began to think about when they would go up, because if they continued that way they would soon reach the peak of the mountain.

- What was that other mark on the map, which looked like a lot? He asked to see if he could find any other information about the route they would take.

- It's "Huaca Apacheta". That we can see with a little more than an hour of walking.

- And what exactly is this "Huaca Apacheta"?

She took a while to answer, half wondering if it was worth it or if she should wait until they arrived and, he would see for himself. She decided to answer, because she knew he wouldn't stop asking until he found out.

- It is an old bridge made by the Incas, whose construction is said to have taken place two hundred and fifty years before the discovery of the Americas.

- A bridge with more than. He stopped to calculate. More than seven hundred years. Concluded. And let me guess: We're going to go through it, right?

- Yes. Due to the short time we have we will have to go there!

- It was all I needed today! A radical crossing to complete my monotonous day.

She didn't respond the way she imagined he deserved, as he was already getting used to his sarcastic way of speaking. He knew that in the end it didn't matter. It was his boring way of being. After that, they walked in silence for a long time, just observing the landscapes and native plants. They reached a point on the slope that the fog was beginning to make the view shorter and they could not see so far. His field of vision had been reduced to about a hundred meters.

As the climate between them had returned to be a little tense, they walked in silence until reaching "Huaca Apacheta". On the way Victor could see a strange terrain where the soil was exposed and it was possible to see that it was composed of several well-defined layers. He then remembered a conversation he had had with a colleague who had told him parts of the story of Charles Darwin's expedition. He recalled some passages in which, while visiting Argentina, he had found parts of fossilized trees. And these trees helped Darwin to analyze, summarize, deduce. I didn't know for sure. He knew that they had contributed to formulating his most famous work: The theory of the evolution of species.

- Can you give me more details about this bridge? He asked, trying to break the ice.

- Well, see for yourself. There she is!

Saying this, she pointed to a spot high in front of her, and in the mist Victor could see two rock pillars about three meters high. Without realizing it, they started walking faster. He couldn't believe what he was seeing. They looked like two Greek porticos without the characteristic carvings. Quickly in his mind the weight of the pieces came up: They certainly reached more than two tons each.

They were at an altitude of more than three and a half thousand meters and in front of them was a valley more than four hundred meters deep, at its deepest point. Connecting the two peaks, the bridge could be seen. Made of rope, apparently from some type of local plant. With finely colored and braided ties. The places to step were made of wood, more precisely of broken logs in half, with the flat part facing upwards. Thus forming a flat support and at the same time non-slip by the exposed fibers. It was strange to imagine a bridge over seven hundred years old in such good condition.

- How can it be so well maintained at all this age? He asked.

- Some people in the village keep it preserved to cross when they need it. Which doesn't happen very often. I think it keeps it preserved for its historical significance.

- And what is this meaning?

- Around here, in the past, there was an old Inca road. Built so that the empire had access to the most remote geographical regions of its vastness. And this bridge saved about a day crossing the valley.

- Interesting. And why did they give this strange name to the bridge?

- "Huaca Apacheta" is not the name of the bridge!

- And what is it then?

- Here it is!

Saying this she pointed to a heap of small stones about a meter high.

- Is that "Huaca Apacheta" over there?

She nodded and he started to laugh.

- Could you tell me how a map can refer to a pile of stones and not a bridge of megalithic proportions?

- Those are not common "pebbles". At least not for the people of the village and others who still follow their customs. Saying this his air became more serious causing Victor to stop laughing. The place marked by these stones is a sacred place for the people. Something special happened to someone at this location. And the natives believe that by leaving a memory they honor the natural spirit that promoted what happened. Each of the stones you can see is the sign of a person who came by and showed his respect. They call these "sacred" places the name Huacas.

- You mean they think there is something sacred in this place?

- It's more or less this.

- And what kind of sacred thing happened here?

- It is not a miracle, as we conceived it. It may have been a vision, a perception, the appearance of a sacred animal, I am not sure. I just know that something different has happened here. People who feel or go through this experience deposit something in memory of it. Then other people who come by and notice the tribute already paid, deposit stones, as it is the only thing they have at the moment. They think that with this they are honoring the sacred and maintaining or expanding their luck in life.

Victor started to think about what he had just heard and again in his mind there were numbers. I was thinking, at that moment, of the amount of stones that should be on that hill. Doing a quick head count, which took no more than fifteen seconds, came to an estimate of approximately twenty thousand pebbles. Twenty thousand people had already passed by and deposited a stone. Not to mention the people who didn't.

The place was covered by undergrowth and the trail had almost disappeared, and this indicated that it had not been that popular for some time. This made him think again: Who were those twenty thousand people? Why did they have to cross over there?

- Let's continue? Estela broke out, breaking his trance.

- Since we have no other option. But you go ahead! And only after reaching the other side will I go, right?

She smiled, was starting to get used to his way. He was programmed for harsh responses and didn't even realize he was being inconvenient. Another comfort he found was that in several of his answers he had gone bad. For when it was needed, she was also very quick to respond.

- Agreed, then! He replied walking towards the bridge.

The bridge was narrow, just over two feet wide. Consequently, it allowed only one person to pass through at a time. He could come right after her, because in his opinion the bridge was very well maintained. But he thought it best not to abuse his luck. She stepped on the first step and heard a creak. It looked like the wood and the ropes were settling in on each other.

- When you come, step in the center of the woods so that the bridge does not lean to the sides and start to swing!

- Right! Thanks for the tip.

Her crossing was very fast and as soon as Victor started to worry when Estela shouted and waved, showing that he was already on the other side.

- Come on, Victor! Don't look down and go at your pace, straight ahead! He said to himself, taking courage.

Then he stepped on the first step, hearing the same creaking sound he had heard less than two minutes ago. He leaned on the side ropes and realized they were damp and very cold. They were certainly like that due to the fog that still covered most of the surrounding peaks. The second step was easier. He took confidence and moved on. He counted fifty-eight steps and that was fine. He stopped for a while to catch his breath and can hear her voice very close, directing him to the arrival.

At that moment he felt a very hot gust of wind from the bottom up, clearing all the fog that surrounded him. He felt the ropes drying and the wood crackling under his feet. He lost his balance for a moment and had to hold on tight. He began to hear the scream of people coming from the side where he had entered the bridge. They seemed to be getting closer by the moment. His concern turned to despair and, forgetting where he was, he dropped the ropes and started running.

Estela looked away for a moment, and turning back to the bridge he noticed that it had been covered by a strange mist. I couldn't see where Victor was anymore. At that moment he felt a great bump on the other side of the bridge, as if an enormous weight had fallen on it. He didn't think for a second: He ran as fast as possible, over the logs. When he reached Victor he was lying down, and only two small ropes prevented him from falling over fifty meters at that point.

She spoke to him, but to no avail, so she tried to turn it over and in doing so she realized that her eyes were glassy and totally white. Like the Elder in the village the first day he had been there. She froze for a few seconds, but realizing that he would fall if she remained still, she decided to wrap a rope around herself and Victor. And then she started to pull him by the hands. It was an exercise in strength, balance and patience. Step by step she took him until they reached the other side. When he passed the stone pillar, he removed the rope from his body and tied it to the pillar.

He splashed some water on his face and lay down to catch the air for a moment. Victor was still static for a few seconds, but gradually regained his consciousness. And coming back to himself, he had involuntary spasms where he seemed to be taking electric shocks. Finally he whispered:

- Estela? Where are you? Stele?

- I'm here. Give me your hand.

She squeezed his icy hand and he could feel the warmth of it passing over his body once again. A few seconds later that bad feeling he had experienced had passed. They exchanged calmer looks at that moment. They were beginning to understand each other better. Victor knew a good part of her story. Estela, for her part, knew that he had much bigger problems than he could have imagined, but he believed that his opportunities were also good.

As if by instinct they started to laugh out loud and when they realized they were laughing. After the shock, it was a very relaxing moment and it seemed to last an eternity.

- Thanks for helping me! Said Victor, stopping laughing. I owe you a lot!

- No problem, after all I was the one who brought you here. And after a brief pause, as if afraid to ask. What happened to you?

- I am not right. But we need to go, don't we? It seemed to disagree. I can tell you the details as we walk. Can be?

She found that attitude strange, but she nodded. They got up and followed the trail that disappeared behind a large rock and started to flank to the right. Now it was easier, because they were going down. Victor thought. During the last hour of walking they talked about what happened on the bridge and it was clear to Estela that he had had a vision. I wasn't sure what it was about, but it was certainly a vision.

Victor, on the other hand, found it strange to be unconscious, since he could see and hear Estela in his apparent dream. I could see countless figures of natives, but Estela was totally preserved and her appearance was the same as that moment, except for the clothes. He began to take an interest in the information she was telling him. About the region, the stories of the village and the local culture. Now that he started to meet them, they seemed quite interesting. They went back up again, reaching the top of a cliff from which they could see far in the distance. Estela stopped for a moment and looked to the North and to her map. He seemed to be in doubt, so Victor asked:

- What's it? We're lost?

- No, but take a look at the map to see if you can help me understand.

He looked and saw that on the map there was the drawing of two mountains next to each other, whose central point when aligned with that stone where they were found formed an imaginary line under which, at the bottom of the valley that followed, the location of the this Indian's house. Next to the site was also the drawing of a waterfall with the words "Caida de la Niebla" written on it.

Observing the mountains, he noticed that there were several landscapes similar to the one on the map. The map seemed a little confused, leaving room for errors. Looking more closely at him you can see that there were details of the terrain around the peaks. It was clear that they were made on purpose, because everything else that appeared was at a lower level, lower than that of the mountains.

Showing that detail to Estela, the two were sure that it was really a very important detail. Looking back to the North, they could distinguish two peaks that were flanked and were slightly higher compared to the others. They looked at each other and nodded and agreed on the peaks.

- Now I only have one question: There are no doubts about the starting point, is there?

- Yes, because on the map it said to follow the trail to the rock.

- Okay and is the North another reference we have?

- Yes, that's it. Although not indicated on the map, the person who handed it to me said it.

- And who is this person?

- I think it is not advisable to go into details.

- Why not?

- Well. Let's say you might not like to hear about these details.

- Before maybe, but I'm changed. Now you can tell me, without any hard feelings.

- I can start by saying that it does not come from a person in a conscious state of thought.

- What? Did you get this from some crazy person?

- Not with a madman! She laughed. The person is very old and was. I think the word is. Unconscious. You know, stuff from local people.

- What? He said, seeming not to believe what he had just heard.

- I asked him for help in his place and told me he needed some time to get help. At the end of the day he came to me with the map and instructions, saying that his problem was bigger than I imagined and we would need someone with more knowledge than he had.

- Nice! We have in our hands a map made by an old junkie, or whatever!

- Don't talk like that! I respect him a lot, and I ask him to respect him too.

He took a walk around himself, kind of recovering his lucidity and said very quietly, almost whispering:

- I'm not sure if I should have come.

- And I'm not sure I should have told you the truth. She said loud and clear.

- Okay, I'm sorry. Let me think for a few minutes that I'll be back to normal soon. Excuse me.

Saying this he started to look in the distance and she decided to focus on what they should do next. He stopped thinking about the way the map had been designed and recreated the image of the line in his mind and followed the line through the ground where he passed to see if he could find any signs that might be the place they were looking for.

He was unable to concentrate and began to disperse again. He almost gave in to disbelief. For a moment he focused on the situation and resumed his analysis. He noticed some medium-sized vegetation forming at the base of the valley and as it was going up, it thinned out until there was only that low grass that they were used to seeing. At some points you can see that there was no vegetation at all, which should be some big rock or the concentration of rock chips, which was also common in those places.

I was looking for some alteration in the landscape that could show the presence of people. A few minutes there and he couldn't see anything that caught his eye. It was at this moment that Estela showed him something from the side of a mountain to the right of the valley. At first he hadn't seen it, but after focusing a little, he could see a very thin white thread that they thought was the stream that probably formed the "Caida de la Niebla". And following the imaginary line with the stream line they reached a point.

- The ladies at the front! He said in response to Estela's gaze.

Both in agreement, strode out towards the point in the landscape that they found a minute ago. Their greatest hope was that they were right.

- I also saw a phrase written on the map several times, but it was in some language I don't know. Do you know what you mean? He asked about half an hour after they left, making conversation.

- I can't understand, but before I left I asked a person in the village. She told me it was an enigmatic phrase that didn't make much sense to her either, but that said something like: "Under the guard of the twelve the last great priest rests, and in the darkness of the meeting between Quilla and Inti he will reveal himself".

- And does that make any sense to you?

- Not until now, that's why I didn't say anything.

- What a strange thing.

He couldn't get it out of his head and started looking at the landscape around him to see if he could notice anything that made sense of that phrase. He started looking for large trees to see if his count was twelve, but there were more than twelve trees in the woods in front of him. Large stones, as in "Stonehenge". This should be it! He started counting the stones and was also disappointed to find the stones he needed in less quantity. There were three or four huge rocks, but the rest of them were infinitely small in size to count.

He stopped for a moment and took a sip of water. He threw some on his hands and brought it to his face. He rubbed his hands over his face and with a movement raised his head, keeping his eyes closed and then opening them. At this moment you can contemplate all the beauty of the two peaks where you were heading. Initially turning his head and then the body went around him completely and when he faced the spikes again, he shouted to Estela who was right in front of him:

- Hey, Estela! I already know the meaning of part of the puzzle.

- Oh yes?! And what did you discover? She asked suspiciously, stopping where she was.

- Look around. She signaled she hadn't noticed anything. Count the peaks surrounding the valley. He said, showing impatience.

And that's what she did. Like Victor, she started by turning her head and continued with her body until she returned to where she started. Her eyes showed excitement, but her words didn't match, as if she didn't want to give him an arm to twist.

- IS! It seems like a possibility.

- "Possibility". I'm sure I'm right! It can only be this!

She smiled in conformation and he knew that she also accepted his hypothesis.

- This indicates that we are in the right place, but it leaves a range of location the same size as the valley. Which still doesn't help much. We will continue to the point that we had drawn.

- Okay, let's go then! But that you liked my discovery, you liked it!

- Of course I liked it. It was an expert thing: To be able to count to twelve and to manage at the same time.

- You can laugh at will, because the taste of victory is mine. He said playfully.

They continued on the trail for a long time and it was already past four hours when a very strong wind started to blow. A few clouds that were above their heads dispersed very quickly. They forgot about the map and their objective for a moment because that sudden change caught their attention. It kept getting dark and they were worried because it was still early in the evening. Estela could not accept that it was already getting dark. At that time the sun was setting close to six o'clock, and there was still more than an hour to go.

The shadows of the rocks and small bushes that were next to them began to oscillate, time being there, time disappearing. A blast of icy wind passed them, and they shook hands tightly. A flock that was supposed to have more than a thousand birds came up the slopes and it looked like it was going to take everything in front of it with it. Victor pointed to the West and Estela did not believe what he was seeing. It looked like a huge shadow coming at an extraordinary speed towards them.

Dread washed over the two who approached and crouched. The night took over the environment and the remaining shadows became even stranger: covering themselves with waves that seemed to flee when they tried to focus on them. They looked at the sun, and saw something forming over it. Frightened for so long, they broke away and only then realized that it was an eclipse.

- It's a total solar eclipse! Estela whispered in awe. Do you have any idea how rare they are?

- "in the darkness of the meeting between Quilla and Inti he will reveal himself". Victor completed without appearing to have paid attention to what she said at the end. What do Quilla and Inti mean?

- Inti means sun in Quechua, but Quilla I can't say.

- "in the darkness of the encounter between the Moon and the Sun it will reveal itself". Victor said out loud for her to hear. He just wasn't as excited as the first discovery, because his heart was racing and his legs were still wobbly.

They remained with their eyes fixed on the sky, and could see the thin edge of light that still remained for the sun to be completely overcast. A few seconds later and the edge was broken, seeming to have something preventing its continuity. In the sequence a ring with intense shine was formed and reminded the shine of a diamond. And the sun seemed to have created an intense mane. The explosion waves that formed the solar winds reminded him of the representations that everyone knew of the Sun. Waves seeming to dance from side to side, being thrown from the surface into space. The darkness changed to a greyish blue and resembled the sunrise. Even the stars were visible.

She regained her lucidity and began to walk the valley looking for any sign to show the whereabouts of the elder Indian, but with that darkness everything seemed to have become even more difficult.

- Can you see anything? He asked.

- I can not see anything. Is that you?

- Neither!

A few seconds later and his eyes were already adapted. They were able to realize again the path they should follow. Just after the point they had imagined as the location, she noticed a luminescent point forming. It was quite tenuous at first, but after a moment of staring he was as sharp as a star in the night sky. And it really looked like a star.

Estela, who was totally focused until that moment, gave a cry of euphoria when she saw the place and searched in vain for Victor, who was no longer at his side. With the intense darkness, I could only see the stars in the sky, and how beautiful they were during the day.

He was afraid and called again for him, and again he got no answer. I needed to find him, but I was afraid of missing the spot. He used an old technique that he learned on television. He took two sticks of similar measures and stuck them in line with each other and whose points when observed coincided with the desired location. He did this and he never stopped calling for Victor.

His concern continued to increase. At this moment he gave thanks, as the luminosity began to return. She felt great relief at that. She was going crazy for losing him. He looked around and noticed something just below where they were. He ran as fast as he could and found him lying face down on the vegetation. He turned his body and realized that he was unconscious again, in a trance. He shook his body and splashed water on his face, but nothing seemed to make him come to himself.

He looked at the sky, towards the Sun, where the bright halo was beginning to lose its intensity. He didn't hear Estela's voice anymore. His gaze could not withstand direct contact with the Sun for a long time, even if partially taken by the Moon. He closed his eyes and moved his head down, as if he wanted to chase away the discomfort caused by the light. When he opened his eyes, he could see many people running desperately everywhere. He was static when he heard the shouting that had taken place and it took him a while to realize that he was no longer with Estela. The place looked like a small square with a dirt floor.

Many people passed him. Most were women who strayed as they approached. Screaming and with small children on their lap. They wore very colorful and trim clothes that looked like big ponchos. In very vivid tones, you could see the large amount of red, brown, green and yellow. They were natives, for sure. They were running like crazy, but you can see they were not going in one direction. They ran from side to side as if they were lost. They seemed terrified of something. Looking further away you can see that some were pointing at him. But the vast majority looked at the sky, spread their arms, shouted something and ran again.

He walked a little so that he had his eyes free and could see where they were pointing when they opened their arms and screamed. He passed a house made of pale stones, probably from the mountains in the region. People's despair was increasing, so he decided to walk faster and see what was happening. He heard the words of the people passing by, but he couldn't understand them. He tried to stay sober in the face of all that rushing, but it was very difficult.

In that instant he heard a loud sound, which sounded like the sound of a bugle. The screaming stopped for an instant. Stately dressed men passed him, dragging a person. He swerved to avoid being hit by the people following the three. He followed behind them and found themselves in a small crowd. In the background, a darker stone table could be seen, slightly higher than the local floor. At the altar a figure covered in gold was waiting. He looked like a priest, wearing a large hat in the shape of a halo, which resembled the rays of the sun.

They held the person dragged on the table. The silence was general and the priest said something that he did not understand again. People started to throw themselves on the floor and commit self-harm. They cut themselves and threw the blood that flowed towards the stone altar. At that moment the priest pointed the knife at the sky, as if consecrating it. At the same time taking the strength to deliver the killing blow. Victor followed his movement when he raised the knife, and when he reached the highest point, he could see the reason for all that uproar. An eclipse was forming and the sun was starting to get dark, partially overcast!

- No! He screamed with all his strength the moment he understood the madness that was about to happen.

He came to himself in time to hear the echo of his scream running through the valley. Estela shook him with all her might and called out her name. He quickly came to himself and jumped to his feet. He looked around and at Estela, who was visibly scared. Her face was covered in sweat, which made her imagine that she had been there for some time, trying to wake him up. Regaining consciousness he asked:

- What happened? How did I get here?

- We were looking to try to find the place of the elder's house, but after a few seconds that the eclipse started you disappeared. I marked the place I saw during the eclipse and went looking for it. After a while I saw something and heard a whisper, followed them and found you. She paused for a moment as if taking the strength to believe what she was going to say.

- Initially you were in a trance, like the last time. But after a while he sat on the floor and, all curled up, mumbled things that I couldn't understand. Suddenly you got up and ran and screamed, stumbling over everything in front of you. I was terrified, thinking it might fall and hurt itself. I tried to follow you, but I couldn't. Soon after you stopped and crouched, starting to cry, hiding your face, as if you were afraid of something. That's when I reached you and started calling you.

He remained silent, as he again tried to assimilate everything that had been happening since that day in the cabin. After taking several deep breaths he took courage and said:

- I had a very strange dream during the situation you described to me. And I don't remember anything you just said to me. He paused, struggling to remember the details.

- Another very strange thing, which may be just another coincidence, is that when I regained consciousness, I looked at the Sun and the Moon had just left its front, ending the eclipse.

He was going to start talking more, but she thought it best to take advantage of the little time they had left, and said:

- You don't have to tell me anything now. We have very little time, so we are going to meet our destination and on the way you will tell me about the dream. It's ok?

He nodded, and the two headed towards the place she had marked.

Seized by the nervousness of the situation, they did not realize that they were being followed. The creature came very close to him in the moment of darkness and almost managed to reach his goal. Luckily, or some other force, he ducked just as she made a low flight to hit him. Now, again in the presence of his father, Inti, he could not attack him.

From the other side of the valley, a figure was watching their actions and had also noticed the creature in pursuit. Seeing that they escaped, he turned back to what he was doing, as he should be prepared when they arrived. Which would take just over an hour.

SEVEN

The descent was much faster, than they were imagining. And except for the countless stones, the terrain helped a lot. But the Sun seemed to have increased its speed after the event: It was moving rapidly to the West and an unconscious fear grew within them. Near the base of the valley there was a small bog that was just over three meters wide, but as it was very shallow, they had no problem crossing it. As for the climb that started next, it seemed that it would not be easy. They came face to face with a huge, steep rock that looked like it couldn't be climbed so they went around. But this took time that they didn't have.

They even had to use the rope they had brought. Victor became very tired after the transposition of the rock. The thin air affected him a lot, even though he chewed coca constantly. Estela, on the contrary, showed no sign of tiredness. The time she lived in the neighborhood was enough for her to be perfectly adapted, like the natives of the region. Still, he often needed the blessed leaves. His look showed concern, not for the way, but for the time that was already.

Victor sat down to get some more air, but she glared at him and he soon got up. At that moment, they could hear the sound of water flowing, as if a small stream ran overhead.

- It could be the stream that comes from the waterfall and if we follow it we can get to the place faster! Estela said excitedly, wanting to believe in the new possibility.

They agreed to follow the stream, as the direction was the same as the location. Her biggest concern was whether they would be able to find the place before sunset. Another fact that also worried her was that she was not sure about the location of her goal. I couldn't assess whether they had progressed well or not on the way. For a while the sound of the wind on the slopes and the whisper of the waters of the stream running towards the great descent was all they could hear.

- How do you think we are? Asked Victor.

- I have no idea! She replied dryly.

- I was just trying to start a conversation, I didn't need to answer this way. He said, venting. I'm also nervous, but I'm trying to dispel my nervousness by talking to you.

She looked around, without thinking much of what he had said and said:

- Don't you think this place is beautiful?

For a moment he was silent, wondering if she had heard what she said and if she would say anything other than that, but as she said nothing else, he replied.

- Yes, it's very beautiful here. All this landscape that we have been going through in the last few hours should surprise anyone who passes through here. I just think it's a shame that we're passing by in these circumstances and in such a hurry. I would like to spend more time here. Camping maybe.

- I have lived in the region for more than three years and I still can't help but be surprised by the richness of the local nature. I think we noticed more at the beginning, when we have a shock with our old visual paradigm. After a while, I think it's normal for that new reality to end up becoming your new paradigm and you no longer notice all that.

He paused, as if reorganizing his thoughts.

- I think I'm rambling too much, right?

- No. I can understand you perfectly. It becomes part of you so naturally that it becomes invisible. So remarkable is this ability that the human being has to adapt.

- That's right. Watch out here! The stone is covered with slime. She pointed to where he should be looking.

He had never valued the little things he had in his life. In fact, he thought that, until that moment, he hadn't had time to feel it. His life was so run over that he couldn't feel what was really behind it. I was beginning to realize the value of things that some call simple, but which are actually the essence of our life. He remembered a moment in his life when he still believed in God, and he imagined that perhaps this was his manifestation, making him learn through the options he had taken.

- When I was a teenager. Estela started. I lived in a big city and I couldn't help noticing and thinking about people who were going through some suffering at that time. I saw street children, people pulling rubble cars, drug addicts. Well, this kind of thing. Since that time, this has left me very frustrated with God and with men. God should intervene in all that evil! And men had to stop harming each other! He paused to catch his breath. I decided that if God didn't do his part, I would help in some way. I chose at that moment what my profession would be. I left behind everything I had planned for my life, I really wanted to make a difference for these suffering people. I also wanted to increase my help efficiency, so I decided to move to some place where I really needed it. I was happy, because I saw a clear reason and why it was worth living and directing my life. For a long time that reality was enough for me to move on.

He paused to confirm the path, after dodging a dry branch.

- At this moment, when I was more certain of my decision, I had an experience of loss, which put in check the power I thought I had over things and situations. Being in a place that could make the difference you thought essential, was no longer such a good option. I almost gave up on all that. I talked a lot with the oldest of Ayllu who taught me something that I never forget and helped me to move on.

He paused again, which made Victor anxious.

- What was this teaching, anyway? And what is Ayllu?

- Well, we talked several times and if I can sum it up, it goes something like this: Despite our efforts we are not totally sovereign over our destinies. We do decide which way to go, but regardless of this choice, the experiences we must live to evolve will be presented to us. Whichever way we decide to go.

- Wow. Really really deep. I need a moment of reflection to assimilate everything that you told me. I am very grateful for trusting me by sharing all this experience. Victor was really surprised by everything he had heard from Estela. Even because I knew I was being very nice and friendly. But you still haven't told me what Ayllu is!

- Ayllu has a similar meaning to the community, group, or the like.

- The village is an Ayllu! How interesting. Similar to a tribe.

- The concept is a little broader than tribe. Completed Estela. It is a community where everyone has some degree of kinship. That is why the union is so strong.

- Are they all related? But how can this happen?

- Actually, everyone considers themselves relatives, but there is the entry of people from other Ayllus and thus the genetic mixture.

- I didn't understand the relationship.

- There in the village everyone considers themselves relatives, because they believe they are descended, in one way or another, from

Mallqui that is present there. She said with fear that he would continue the investigation.

- Mallqui? Why don't you tell me everything you know at once, to see if I can understand.

- Okay, let's start from the beginning then. An Ayllu is created with the aim of the collective work of the land by a community. And for this community to have a greater bond than work, it receives a divinity that will take care of everyone. The divinity is called Mallqui and everyone venerates him, as it maintains the balance of crops, livestock, land and rain. Mallqui is given the obligations and rights of residents.

- I understood the concept, but it is still not clear to me what this Mallqui is. Estela seemed reluctant to speak to him, but saw that as long as he did not tell her the questioning would not stop. And how can they be descended from a deity?

- Mallqui is the mummy of the first recognized ancestor in the community. And his astonishment was immediately noticed.

- I do not know if I understand. Did you say mummy?

- Yes, a mummy.

- But I imagined that there were only mummies in Egypt.

- A common mess! In the past, all Ayllus had a mummy that community members worshiped. Today, due to the religious imposition of the Spaniards, only a few keep their mummies.

- Is there a mummy in the village?

- Yes, there is. But I think we should go back to our search. Then we can talk more about Ayllu.

When they looked at their watch, they saw that it had been half an hour since they left the base of the valley. The map they had would be of no help at that moment, as it was on a much larger scale than they needed in that part of the journey. But Estela had a very good sense of direction and was already locating herself again so they could move on.

Victor took advantage of the short stop to drink water directly from the stream. That on that stretch formed a small drop from where water could be more easily drunk.

- Do you see that forest? Asked Estela, pointing to a strip that immediately hid a rise in the ground.

- Yes. It seems a long way from here and from the place we imagined. Do not you think?

- I think there should still be around two kilometers by then. But if we go around in that direction we can take about half to get there, as this climb is very steep and rocky.

- If you think that's where we should go, then let's go.

They drove in the direction of the forest for more than forty minutes. They didn't say anything else until then. Her for being focused on the goal and him for still reflecting on everything she had told him. At this point they had another problem to solve: A small lake was forming in front of them. They had not seen him because he was covered by bushes and below his location. It was fed by a slightly larger stream that they were following and to follow they would have to cross it. Estela went up the stream a little and found a point where they could cross without any major problems.

They resumed the direction of the forest in a few minutes and the loss of time that seemed inevitable was much less than they imagined. After that the path improved a lot and they managed to reach the edge of the forest in less than half an hour. Before crossing the forest they decided to make a quick stop and eat some more. The sun was already touching the snow-capped peaks and shadows were beginning to fall on the slopes. They needed to step up. And they needed to do this quickly.

In the woods where the shadows moved, covering the environment, a non-human figure followed them. Stealthily from bush to bush, from stone to stone, like a predator preparing to attack its prey. The stones and shrubs were not able to hide it, but it was his instinct and there was no way to fight it. A natural and almost inevitable programming, similar to the programming that I had started to execute a long time ago, when it was conceived.

Victor ate and drank very little, as far as she could tell. But as they were in a hurry, it wasn't very strange. They barely finished eating and he, for the first time, took the lead on the walk. They entered the small forest, which was strangely darkened. With just under five minutes of walking inside, Victor ducked quickly, as if he were dodging something. Estela, who was right behind him, was startled by the thought that he might have been bitten by an insect. When she looked at him again, she saw him running away. Without deviating from the branches and rolling over the rocks and small bushes on the way. At the same time Estela went after him, but he seemed very determined in his run. It seemed that his life depended on that rush. And maybe it really did.

Entering the forest, a series of natives surrounded him and started something like an interrogation. Victor, in a moment of distraction from one of the natives, had managed to bend down, steal a spear and run away. And that was what was going on now. A bunch of fierce natives who were chasing him and certainly didn't want to talk to him. He remembered Estela and looking back he could only see the figures of his pursuers. He wanted to go back, but something bigger than his will didn't allow.

After running like crazy after Victor for more than fifteen minutes, and not reaching him, Estela got very tired and gave up on the chase. He started walking, concentrating on following the sounds of the steps he made when running, which were not at all subtle. Shortly afterwards the sounds also disappeared and what was left for her was just an idea of the direction to follow. He noticed a trail of dented bushes that he had left behind. Through these bushes and stones, he was sneaking around hoping to find him at any moment.

It still amazed him that it was so dark under those small trees. Another thing that also caught his attention was the cold that he suddenly started to get. I knew they had at most another half hour of sunlight, so they would be exposed. And if what Ayllu's people had said was right, they would be easy targets. For this reason I needed to find him as quickly as possible and hope he was conscious. Thus they would resume the path.

The closer they got to their destination, the more it seemed that Victor was lost in his trances. A strange coincidence, she thought. I was curious and intrigued by the whole situation. Deep down what it looked like was that his subconscious was active and trying to escape the danger that followed him. As in the case of a prey that when attacked runs without knowing the reason, but the adrenaline in its bloodstream speaks louder. Your instinct! Instinct again!

But there was no time for this now, I had to move on. Almost as suddenly as they entered the woods she came out of it. As he crossed a large trunk and dodged a huge stone, the light reappeared, blinding his vision for an instant. You can feel the more muffled breath of air on your face. When you regain sight, you can distinguish a figure moving in front of you, slightly to the right. Her heart beat faster. I had finally found it. He started running towards the figure, but he was way ahead of him and moving fast. It would be very difficult to achieve it and when I did, I thought I was still beside myself.

He reached a point where he had to go around a small rocky slope and ended up being distracted. As he went around the slope, he tried to locate Victor, but failed. He called by his name, but there was no sign in response. He paused for a moment to try to listen more carefully to help him decide which way to go. Looked around. Behind her was the strange forest. He thought he might still be there, hurt or unconscious. That maybe I hadn't seen anything.

He began to think that that adventure might have been meaningless. It was something they could have resolved otherwise. They could run away, for example. He ran his hand over his face to regain his lucidity, and felt his throat and stomach tighten inside. The sensation was almost uncontrollable and he knew that crying did not help anything, but he cannot control himself. He fell to the ground, as if the whole sky was weighing tons on his shoulders and burst into tears.

She wanted him to appear suddenly, and everything was as simple as if they were in a restaurant and he came back from the bathroom. He got up, wiped his tears and started walking.

- Head in the direction where you had seen the figure! She told herself.

He crossed another small stream of crystalline waters, where moss-covered stones surrounded him. Looking down from where he was trying to cross, he realized what he thought was a mark on the rock, where the moss was pulled out. Was it a shoe brand ?! He wasn't sure, but it was in the direction she was pointing. A little ahead, almost imperceptible because it is covered with long grass, you can clearly see the footprint of a newly made shoe. Now he was sure: Victor had passed by!

And it wasn't that long ago. Victor's trail now showed itself to her again. He was filled with hope and started running down the path, sure that he would soon find him. He passed several crushed bushes and a large broken branch. Up ahead, on your right, about fifty meters away, you can see what looked like a small rise in the terrain, but it did not immediately attract her attention.

He stopped looking around again and had a strange sensation when he passed the elevation of the terrain. It looked like a very old Huaca, on which the vegetation began to bloom and cover the stones offered. He thought that maybe he was dizzy because a rock behind Huaca, seemed to have moved. She narrowed her eyes, not believing what she had seen. It was static and focusing in the direction of Huaca you can see a large part of the terrain moving. It wasn't vertigo! His eyes did not believe what they were seeing and he closed them to see if he could distinguish whatever was moving.

It remained static, petrified! Not willingly, but involuntarily. It was certainly not human. But what could it be? I had no idea. Suddenly the figure jumped on a rock in front of her and she could see it clearly. He looked like a cat-bird mix. It also had a long tail, which kept whipping in the air while the creature seemed to assess its next movements.

It was filled with intense dread. Her body wanted to collapse to the floor so the animal wouldn't see her. She started to lower herself slowly, hoping she wouldn't be seen. At this moment, as if it had been activated by the fear she was feeling, the animal turned to Estela. Their eyes met and she could see a red glow in the bottom of the animal's eyes. They were a light red, looking like cherries. They had an intensity that was capable of causing doubt in the heart of any human being. Estela ran away. I was already prepared to be attacked.

The creature, in turn, fixed its gaze like a bird of prey and, lifting its head, made a very strange noise and also ran at full speed. The sound was something like an eagle and a cat screaming at the same time. Estela ran further, believing that the animal was coming after her. He didn't have time to see anything else. Seconds later everything went black, and the sensation of vacuum only ended when intense pain ran through his body.

Victor, who was still running away from the natives, heard a buzz coming towards him and only had time to move his head to the left, feeling the wind in his ear, and watching the arrow hit the tree in front of him. The energy with which it came was so strong that it shattered the instant it touched the tree. His opponents were many and if he gave up he thought he would be captured or killed, regardless of the order in which this occurred. It ran for another stretch. I wasn't sure how long I was going to endure that pace. He was sweating a lot and his breathing was very fast.

His instinct was being overcome by tiredness. The fastest I could run was no longer enough and I was starting to realize this. He had to devise another strategy or he would be caught. When he couldn't take any more running, he stopped and suddenly ducked, entering a hole in the ground. He pulled out a plant with great foliage and covered himself. His ears were still attentive to the sounds the environment made, trying to hear the noise of the natives arriving. For a few minutes his breathing, so fast, prevented him from hearing everything around him and imagined that he had managed to escape from his pursuers. Part of his energy recovered, his breathing normalized and he began to look around him.

This place was not foreign to him. He seemed to know some trees there. At that moment he heard sounds of the forest moving far away. He stopped in silence, without even breathing. He had no choice but to run again and began to visualize the direction in which he was going. It was very strange, but one of the directions seemed familiar. And decided to go there. The sound started to get closer and the time for your run too. He recovered his energies and took another deep breath.

He dashed off, using the last forces he had left. He jumped on a large log and then on a rock. He sneaked by a kind of hawthorn that scratched his shore. He felt his feet soak and freeze, probably from running over a stream. The darkness was almost total and the little he could see were figures passing by as he ran. Your hands have become your eyes. He hadn't heard anything for a while and thought they had given up.

At that moment an intense pain took over his right leg and he felt as if his flesh had been cut through the back. He fell to the ground and when looking at his leg he saw an arrow with gold ornaments and made of darkened wood, embedded in it. His tiredness and pain were extreme. Her heart sped up and she felt a strange smell around her. The smell was very strong! He felt nauseous, but he didn't know if it was pain, fear or a bad smell. A moment later, a loud roar was heard. As with Estela, everything went dark for Victor.

- At least now I can rest in peace! It was his last thought.

The old Indian was hiding in his hut, curiously watching everything that was going on. His gaze alternated from one to the other without missing a single detail. When he noticed the creature approaching, he was sure he should act. As much as they were two strangers, life was a far more valuable asset than whether or not you knew a person. He ran to an inner part of the hut and picked up a small earthenware vase with rock designs, but with a well-defined symbol in the center: a golden sun.

He left his hut almost as quickly as he took the vase, and a moment later he was already very close to the man, for it was he who was being chased at that moment. He walked around behind Victor, who was in a way he knew very well. So he thought it best not to approach him yet. Twenty meters below it, right in the path that the creature had to pass to catch it, there was a rock big enough for it to hide and wait for it. I wasn't sure if the contents of the jar would work, but I would try anyway. It was the first and only one ever made and was more than six centuries old.

He got dirty with the slime of the rocks to disguise his smell and climbed on the stone, squatting. Anyone looking in your direction would claim that there was a small bush on the rock. He knew he couldn't open his eyes or the creature would certainly notice him, so he should keep his other senses on the alert. He rested his hands well on the rock to feel the movement of the animal's steps. His ears were ready and they canceled all other sounds in the room to focus on the animal's noise. From that moment on, everything was happening in slow motion for him.

The animal was very large, as he soon felt its steps. But it was still a long way off, because the noise of leaves and branches being broken was far away. He counted the seconds in his mind. His heart, instead of racing, slowed. He was an excellent hunter since he was very young and was already used to that sensation: the seconds before the fatal blow.

The sound of the bushes was increasing and the vibration of their footsteps was approaching. Just a few more steps and it would be where he needed it. At this point the animal stopped. I didn't know why, but I had to wait for him to resume his march to act. He started to feel anxious, and he wanted to open his eyes.

- No! Be patient! He told himself.

He waited a few more seconds and nothing. She started to wonder if he hadn't discovered it and was in doubt between following or fleeing. At this moment, a great howl made the Indian open his eyes. He felt a great breath of air at that moment. Something very big had gone over him, flying or gliding, he wasn't sure. He was hit and knocked over the top of the rock.

He turned quickly and managed to hold on to an old root on the side of the rock, falling over a small bush.

The animal's strides streaked ahead of him, towards Victor. He got up at once and took off in the direction the animal had gone. Now her heart was racing. He was still holding the vase, because even after the fall he had managed to protect the vase from breaking. Ten strides ahead, the animal lay still, just moving its neck. The Indian threw the jug from behind on his feet, which broke at the same moment, releasing an odor that took over the entire environment.

The animal put aside what it was doing and turned to the Indian, staring at him for a moment. He was visibly uncomfortable. He swirled around his own body and shook his head with another hellish howl. The tallest of all. The old Indian felt his ears hurt and closed his eyes. He protected himself with his hands, because at the same moment of the cry the animal advanced on him in a jump that he imagined was his end. The soft breath of air that followed the attack was, contrary to what I expected, a sensation that was quite pleasant.

Her heart was racing even after she was sure the animal was gone. For a few seconds he was only able to worry about himself. He forgot the man and woman who had gone out to help. But when he heard a groan coming from the ground, a little ahead, he came to his rescue.

He was about to discover that what was there was not pleasant to see.

MAPS AND FIGURES

INDIANS CAVE

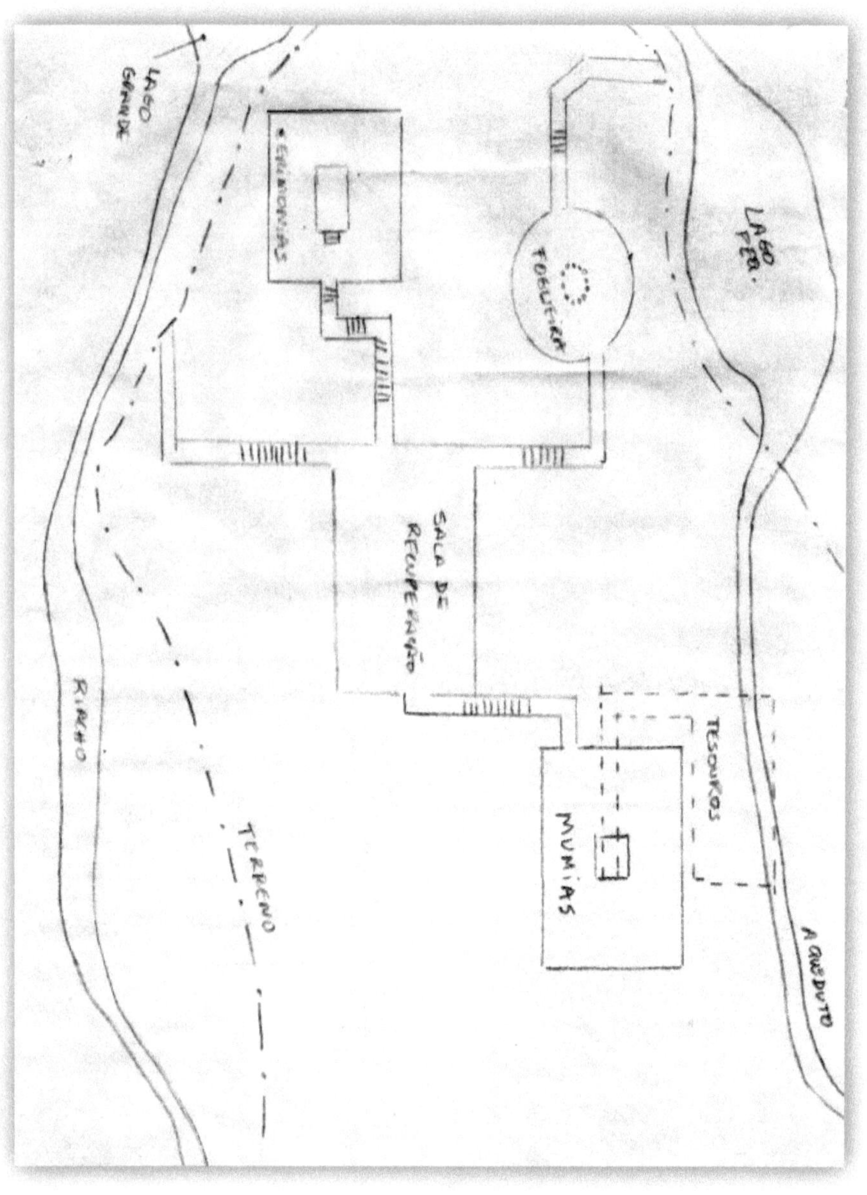

TAHUANTINSUYO

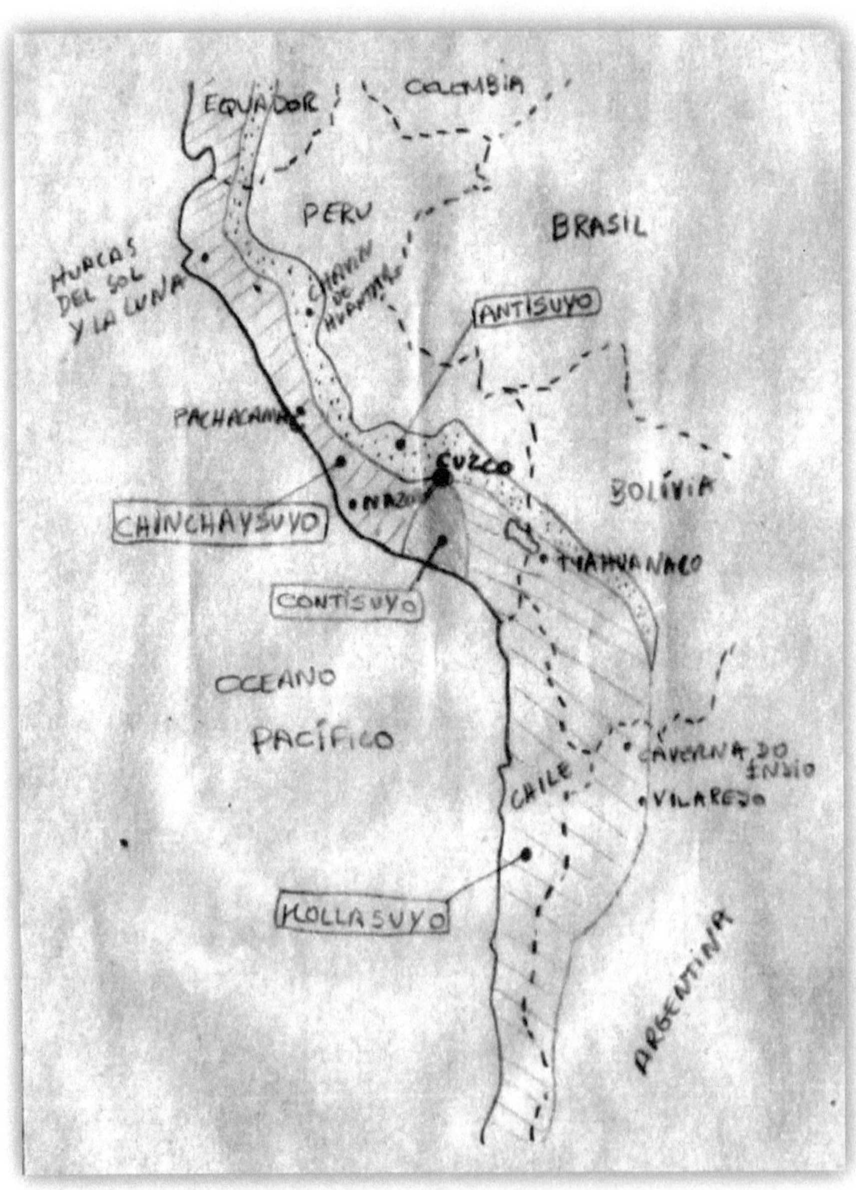

INDIAN REPRESENTATION OF WARI